ABOUT TH

John Madeley is an author, writer and broadcaster, specialising in development and environmental issues. He has travelled extensively in developing countries, including the six countries that feature in this book. "Let Live" is John's second novel. His first, "Beyond Reach?" told the story of the Make Poverty History campaign.

Books by John Madeley:

Beyond Reach? Make Poverty History - the novel
Big Business, Poor Peoples. How Transnational Corporations Damage the World's Poor
50 Reasons to Buy Fair Trade, (co-author)
100 ways to Make Poverty History
A People's World: Alternatives to economic globalization
Food for All: the need for a new agriculture
Hungry for Trade: how the poor pay for free trade
Trade and the Poor: the impact of international trade on developing countries
Land is Life: land reform and sustainable agriculture, (co-editor)
When Aid is No Help: how projects fail and how they could succeed

Details on: www.JohnMadeley.co.uk

The characters, incidents and dialogues in this book are fictitious, the product of the author's imagination. Any resemblance to anyone living or dead is entirely coincidental. It is set in the first six months of 2007.

Published in 2011 by Longstone Books,
19 Barnard Road, London SW11 1QT

A catalogue record for this book is available from the British Library.

Cover by Katherine Baxter

Printed and bound by ImprintDigital.net

Printed on paper made from trees sourced from well-managed, certified forests

ISBN 978-0-9568344-1-6

Let Live

A bike ride, climate change and the CIA

John Madeley

Longstone Books Ltd
London

Comments on John Madeley's first novel, Beyond Reach?

A revealing story about a scandal of our time, witty, sharp – and above all urgent – *Rosie Boycott*

A gripping and inspiring story of forbidden love and the struggle for justice. In a hundred years people will look back on our culture of greed and realise books like this helped change the world – *David Rhodes*

In this amusing novel, John Madeley links modern ethics and politics with the age-old issues of relationships and the meaning of life. All this, with serious intent, too – *Tim Lang*

A challenging and absorbing read – *Womanalive*

Truly a great marriage of entertainment and purpose. Compulsory reading for all teachers in training and ordinands – *Peter Wedgwood*

A timely love story that engages the reader's interest from the outset..... will keep you turning pages to the end. Highly recommended for both readability and relevance! – *Steve Rollins*

Most satisfying is the thorough research – *Church Times*

A story rarely told... of what it is like to be a local campaigner. Manages to highlight the reality of government positions and manoeuvring too often neglected in many accounts, fictional or otherwise. An enjoyable read – *The Networker*

A real thriller - *Jeff Alderson*

Beyond Reach? is a wonderful tribute to all those ordinary people who take action against the scandal of global poverty - *John Hilary*

Asks searching questions about relationships, the nature of love and the meaning of life - *Christian Aid News*

An activist's guide to setting up a campaigning organization - *New Internationalist*

In the tradition of Saturday, this outstanding novel weaves together the world of public events with the private world of individual lives - *Carl Rayer*

I finished the book inspired to keep fighting poverty - *Richard Canning*

Be warned, this book could change your life - *Ann Pettifor*

Dedication

The book is dedicated to people who are suffering from the effects of climate change, and to those who are working to halt the process.

1

Two worlds. David Fulshaw could not wait to get away. "Nothing compares to the simple pleasures of a bike ride, John F Kennedy is reputed to have said. Wow, and here's a guy, thought David, who had made love to hundreds of women, including Marilyn Monroe. And nothing, nothing, compares to cycling. So I've missed nothing, he mused, as his Air France flight touched down in the westernmost point of Africa, Dakar in Senegal, just a few days into 2007. Although he wasn't totally convinced.

As David stepped through the cabin door, humidity slapped him in the face. A long, sweaty queue at passport control followed. Making his way to the baggage carousel in the cramped collection hall, he witnessed a scene as chaotic as the temperature was high. The baggage that David chiefly wanted to see was his steed for his African journey, his bicycle. But on cycling holidays in France, he had flown Air France before with his bike, and knew how to pack it well, pedals off, handlebars turned round, etc. And sure enough it came along, although his bags took an achingly long time.

At customs he got suspicious looks and questions but they seemed to mark him down as *excentrique* rather than up to no good and let him through. Finding what he thought was a quiet corner he put his pedals back on, turned the handlebars the right way round and assembled his bags on his rear pannier carriers. A lightweight instant-erect tent and sleeping bag were the bulky items, otherwise he was travelling light. Very light, considering he was planning to be there for around half the year.

The airport corner he had chosen turned out to be anything but quiet, as sellers of a vast range of items found him and constantly interrupted his re-assembling by badgering him to buy their wares. Saying 'no thanks' a hundred times led to his patience wearing thin.

A 17 kilometre ride to the centre of Dakar was the start of his African journey. The start of 'time out' from normal. Six months in Africa, cycling much of the time, otherwise travelling by other means and maybe just mooching. Time to think, to gaze, to learn, to go deeper, his editor at the London Daily Chronicle had said. After ten years as environment correspondent with the Chronicle, he needed a break from the regular routine.

The paper needed a break. David's articles had won awards and were annoying people in high places. His editor liked that. But he also took the view that David needed to get away from his regular habit of popping on a plane, going somewhere for a week or two and writing instant stories. It was time for him to step back and get more of an on-the-spot feel for what he was writing about.

He should travel deep into the rural areas, his editor told him, talk to people who never make the news, find out more about their lives, their hopes and fears, their needs, get a better understanding of what was going on. It was a time for him to reflect more deeply on what he was writing about, and to come back with new insights, new thinking. And he should take the first half of 2007 to do it. For his first three months away, said the editor, the paper did not want so much as an e-mail from him.

Knowing that David was a cyclist, the editor suggested that he take a bike. He quoted Einstein: "I thought of that while riding my bicycle."

As David loved nothing more than being on his bike, he needed little persuasion. He had joined the Chronicle in his mid-20s, coming from a regional paper where he managed to get himself noticed with a number of stories on the environment. But he had begun to write stories on the environment at university.

In his late 1980s university days, the environment was just taking off as an issue. Behind a word that sounded boring, and some environmentalists who seemed off-putting, there was a growing sense that this was about the quality of life, the future of everyone. That private affluence was fine but that it was marred by increasing pollution, worsening air quality, dirtier rivers, beaches and seas. Private affluence, public squalor, just about summed it up.

The likely effects of the world's heavy use of energy were becoming apparent. And in 1987 came a report which David thought would lead to action. The grandly-named World Commission on Environment and Development served notice that the time had come to take the environmental as well as the economic on board. It talked of the need to achieve sustainable development that meets the needs of the present without compromising the ability of future generations to meet their needs. That meant not ruining the earth today.

The report said that the world was threatened by serious global environmental problems that were leaving increasing numbers of people poor. It spoke of the consequences for people, especially for the poor, of acid rain, the hole in the ozone layer, the spread of the desert. It told of how another 21 million hectares of land were under threat each year -- and, not least, it warned of greenhouse gas emissions and global warming.

It said that some of the policies being pursued by governments threatened people's survival, even the survival of the human race. It called for immediate action.

The report was one of the most important documents ever produced on the future of the world. But when David Fulshaw read it in 1987 he barely realised that government's idea of 'action' was to do nothing much at all for several years. European governments made only sympathetic noises, while the response of the United States barely registered.

But it was local stories that occupied him in his early years of journalism. The incinerator near the village green that should not have been there, the threat to children's health from a rubbish disposal tip near their school, the throwaway society and the problems it was causing. There was no lack of stories, and David wrote well enough to be invited to join the national Daily Chronicle and cover environmental issues for them.

At first it was domestic stories in the UK he covered. But his girlfriend Carol, a journalist on another part of the paper, suggested that he might think further afield, that there were stories in Africa, Asia and Latin America that could interest British readers. But the paper's editor was not convinced.

"I'll work on him for you," said Carol. And work on him she did, with little success. But David was then invited by an aid agency to go to West Africa. The editor grudgingly gave his agreement. It was a visit that changed David Fulshaw's life.

From West Africa he told the stories of people who had nothing, who were battling against enormous odds, struggling to grow food in the face of sand that was drifting onto their land from the Sahara desert. He made the stories vivid and exciting enough to win an award. And for the editor to recognise that were stories in Africa, in Asia and elsewhere that would interest readers. And to tell David that he should spend part of his time abroad.

"Talk to the aid agencies, talk with experts, diplomats, academics, above all with ordinary people," his editor had told him, "read, watch the international news and find good stories. Get yourself there and write. And tell it through people, always people, not through conferences or institutions. It's people, their lives, struggles and aspirations that our readers want to hear about. And keep your jabs topped up."

David took the advice. He read, travelled and met people. For the next eight years he travelled through Africa, Asia, the Middle East and Latin America, talking with people for whom climate change was far more than a theory. Rather it was something that was wrecking their lives.

* * *

Two worlds. Farna Gomis was being forced to go away. As she gently lowered her old and battered bucket down the deep well in her West African village, something was missing.

The rope on the handle of Farna's bucket was long, very long. Down and down went the bucket until Farna's hand was far outstretched down the well...in the hope, in the expectation...of water. But the familiar tug, the bucket becoming heavier as it filled up, was not there.

Farna peered down the long shaft, but could see nothing. The well, that since anyone could remember had yielded water for her ancestors, her parents and her own family, was dry. There was nothing there. The water was gone. Farna knew what that meant. The well of life, the well that had enabled so many people to live, had become the pit of death.

"Ding, dong, bell, pussy's in the well," a rhyme she had heard on the radio went unaccountably through Farna's mind. We are all in the well, she thought, all in the pit, the pit of deep despair.

Farna pulled up the empty bucket, one of her family's few possessions, on a hot and humid day, and sat at the side of the well and wept. Silently. Tears for her family. They had no water. And without water, they had no life. Farna was aware that in some African languages the word for 'water' and the word for 'life' are the same. Water is life; in Swahili, the word for water is 'maji'. Water is magical in its nature.

The sun was just rising over her village, a village deep in West Africa's Senegal, as Farna trudged the mile or so back home. But Farna knew that the sun was setting on the life of her family in that village. In the dusty, arid landscape, all around lay withered crops and stunted trees. No rain. There had been no rain to speak of in the area for three long years. Life was becoming not just intolerable but impossible.

Yet only a decade ago it was so different. Life in the village used to be good, there was a health centre and a thriving school where Farna had learned to read. They generally had enough to eat, although there were sometimes shortages between harvests. Their village was green, they did not have much rain, but rain fell nonetheless in two seasons a year, a long and a short season. But the short season rains had dwindled and then to their alarm, completely disappeared. And the long season rains were not what they were. The impact on their crops was serious. The rain was the only water that most of their crops received. Irrigation for people in their village was totally beyond their means. Over Farna's lifetime, the situation had become worse, much worse.

They used to have occasional droughts, perhaps once every ten years, her father had told her. But in Farna's lifetime, it had become once every three years, and then every other year. Now, there had been no rain for three years.

When Farna was a girl she learnt at school that her country lay in the Sahel region of Africa, a wide stretch of semi-arid land running east-west from the Atlantic ocean to the north-east of Africa, along the southern border of the Sahara desert, and north of wetter areas on the African coast. Farna liked that, liked that she lived in a region called the Sahel. It gave an identity. She learnt the name Sahel accurately describes where this area is located because it is an Arabic word for 'border' or 'margin'.

Farna was also told at school that the Sahel is one of the poorest regions of the world, but that did not mean very much at the time.

As a girl, Farna remembered that her family used to grow maize, and also crops such as cucumber, watermelon and cowpea. All were foods they enjoyed. But the crops need water to grow, reliable rainfall in their growing season. As the rains became erratic and lighter so the maize crop one year failed completely. They went hungry, but they coped. They had ways of coping, of adjusting to what was going on. They were advised to plant sorghum instead of maize, as sorghum is a crop that copes better with drought. They did not enjoy sorghum as much, and neither did it yield as well as maize, but it never failed them like maize.

But then the weather became drier still and even their sorghum fields were not yielding enough to feed them. So they switched to millet. This did not need to grow for as many months as sorghum, it yielded its crop more quickly and was better for dry conditions. It just did not taste as good.

And Farna had heard on the radio that in Britain, millet was regarded as a bird food. "What have we come to," she thought, "reduced to eating bird food." And even the millet harvests were getting smaller. Lack of water was turning fields into deserts.

After the harvest, people used to store some of their grain, either in the ground in big holes, or in circular, thatched barns that were raised from the ground to try to keep pests at bay. They might sell a little of the harvest to give themselves cash for other things. But the situation had become so bad that there was nothing to sell, virtually nothing to store for very long. They needed to eat what they grew. But they were only growing enough for eight or nine months of the year. They were hungry and weak for the remaining months.

Lack of food was bad, but lack of water, thirst, was even worse. Without water Farna knew that her family could not live, not them nor the animals or the plants. And it was getting hotter. Temperatures seemed to rise each year. To cope with the heat, they needed more water, not less, not just the family but also their animals. But over the last three years they had lost most of their livestock, their sheep and goats dying of thirst. Farna felt, at times, as if she wanted to die with them. She felt that she was living in a region of death.

And with no rain to dampen the ground, there came the dust. In the now dry and arid plains, the wind carried columns of dust above the trees. In her village, all they had left was a well that was shared with another village, and a ditch used by all the people in the village. Everyone had to form a line at the well and it often took hours. Water could be bought, but the villagers were subsistence farmers and rarely had money. Many had already left the village, the school was down to a few pupils, the community was dying.

"What's going on?" Farna had asked a worker from an aid agency.

"All over the world the climate seems to be changing," the aid worker had replied, "the world is getting warmer and rainfall more erratic and less frequent in some areas. The cause appears to be an increase in carbon dioxide emissions into the atmosphere. Carbon dioxide, known as a greenhouse gas, has a greenhouse, warming effect on the world."

"It is Western countries who are mostly responsible for these emissions," she had added. "The United States emits 25 per cent of these greenhouse gases and yet has only 5 per cent of the world's population."

It did not seem fair to Farna that her family was suffering because wealthy people far away were emitting all those gases, and that her family's life was in jeopardy as a result. They faced having to pay the price for someone else's carbon emissions, and the price was high. They were being forced out of their village. Forced out by lack of water. Forced eviction. Force.

Tradespeople, water sellers, would come to the village selling water. But with no money for water, Farna sometimes begged for the water seller to lend her money to buy water, just for the day. He always refused. "Farna," he said, "you have no means of paying back." She said she would sell something, do anything, to buy water. "Anything?" the water seller had enquired. Before Farna could even answer, he had moved on with a shrug.

2

Senegal. The road surface into Dakar was good as David made his way from the airport past small roadside houses, shambas, farmsteads, with children milling around, chickens running across the road, sand blowing everywhere, and large vehicles thundering past him, belching fumes. He was thankful for the eye shields he had been advised to wear.

The journey had taken some planning. He hoped to travel through eight African countries. For most of them he would need a visa. He was used to the visa routine. His paper employed a specialist company to lodge visa applications with the High Commission or Embassy in London and then collect them several days later. His editor had agreed that David could use the service for his African journey. As getting just one visa could often take a week, he had started the process of getting them a good two months beforehand.

He had trained for the ride by going out at weekends with a local Cyclists' Touring Club group. Fifty miles at first went up to 70 and 80 and gave him the confidence, misplaced he thought at times, that he could manage his planned ride in Africa.

The bicycle and the route had taken some thought. His dream was to cycle through three countries in West Africa, from Senegal, through Mali and then to Abidjan in Ivory Coast, Côte d'Ivoire. After this he would travel by train, bus or maybe even fly to Kenya where he could get on the bike again to head for South Africa, through Zambia and Zimbabwe, maybe picking up part of a cycle route from Cairo to Cape Town. And he wanted to stay with a university friend in Nairobi who worked for an aid agency.

He knew that he would be traveling on both good surfaces and dirt tracks and could be covering the best part of 4000 kilometres. He realised it could be shorter than that. For this was not an endurance test, he had decided. He would cycle when he felt like it, taking at least one day a week out of the saddle, more if he needed it. And he brought with him a large fold-up bag with a handle into which the bike would go, with wheels and pedals off. This meant he could take a train, a bus, whatever, and it could double as a body cover for nights spent in his tent. It was a tent just large enough to take both cyclist and bike. There would be nothing worse than having his bike stolen.

As the bike would take some pounding he bought a new one, it cost him around £1000, but he felt the investment would pay off. It was strong, but not heavy, with front and rear suspension, and also with stout tyres that he hoped would withstand cycling's downside, punctures. He had brought with him a number of spare inner tubes, and some wheel spokes. He also had a lightweight dynamo fitted to the bike in case something happened that kept him out after dark, and a torch and small radio. It was a radio that was to have dramatic significance.

Language could be a problem. English and reasonably good French would see him through most of the journey. But in isolated areas, where only local languages were spoken, there could be difficulties. He knew, however, from his previous experience of Africa, that in most rural areas it was a good idea to seek out a school teacher who could speak French or English, and also the local language.

He planned the cycle part of the journey carefully, deciding to aim at an average of about 80 kilometres a day, some 50 miles. A modest distance, but on many days he would be riding in temperatures of over 30 degrees. And, especially in West Africa, there would be draining humidity that sapped the energy. Here he would be cycling through the hot, dusty and dry Sahel. Again, he knew from previous experience that he could only expect to do about two-thirds of what he did at home.

He was warned that security could be a problem. He could be mugged, he could be attacked by wild animals. For muggers, a friend had suggested, only half-joking, that he carry a snake with him in a small box. The snake would reside in the box and frighten a would-be mugger -- who would very likely disappear rather quickly at the sight of a snake. It was an idea that David dismissed. For both muggers and wild animals, a pepper spray was his chosen alternative.

Mosquitoes would certainly be a problem. He would be bitten, he risked getting malaria. David had contracted malaria before and knew that if he went down with it, then his bike ride could be wrecked. A mosquito net was a must, as well as the usual anti-malaria tablets and the precaution of covering up after dark when mosquitos were especially active. He wanted to ride at a pace that would allow him to appreciate where he was going, to talk with people on the way and immerse himself as much as he could in the culture of the area he was cycling through. He was not out to prove anything. He was there to get to know African people better, maybe to talk about how climate change was affecting them, and to enjoy his time off from routine. And to be flexible, very flexible, if things turned out differently.

During his travels with the Daily Chronicle, David had seen that climate change was happening and making life harsher for the poor. It was adding to their existing problems making a living. Their ability to cope was strained by factors such as economic globalisation and HIV/AIDS, and now by climate change. And there were close connections.

Globalisation, the world as a single market, meant that more goods and people were being flown and shipped around the world. It led to the use of more fossil fuel and more emissions of greenhouse gases.

A dramatic increase in erratic weather, notably floods and droughts, was being seen, with thousands dying and millions made homeless as a result. Three times the number of disasters were occurring in the 1990s as in the 1960s, said the Red Cross. It warned that disasters that were once likely every 100 years could soon be happening every 25 years.

Experts were saying that for the last 30 years, the countries of the Sahel region had experienced significantly lower rainfall and endured widespread degradation of land in the southern fringes. Livelihoods had become even more difficult. Worsening poverty was the inevitable result.

By the end of 2006, David Fulshaw, nudging 40, dark, single, a relationship with long-time girl friend Carol now over, had visited over 50 developing countries. But he faced a dilemma -- his flying was contributing to the climate change that he was writing about. Yet he had to write from first hand. Where the balance lay was something he wrestled with.

On New Year's Eve 2006, David signed off routine work for six months with a column in the paper which explained why he felt so strongly about climate change.

"Let's be clear, the world is facing a crisis and it's the poor who will suffer most, and indeed are already suffering. The Intergovernmental Panel on Climate Change, a body made up of the world's leading climate scientists, projects that the earth's average surface temperature could rise by up to almost six degrees Celsius over the next 100 years.

"The panel concludes that this would result in water shortages in the arid and semi-arid land areas in southern Africa, the Middle East and southern Europe, lower food output in many tropical and subtropical countries, especially areas in Africa and Latin America already threatened by land degradation and desertification. Tens of millions of people are at risk from flooding and landslides. The earth is in danger of being laid to waste by human folly. We are exploiting it beyond the natural boundaries. Africa, the world's poorest region, is the continent most vulnerable to the impact of climate change because widespread poverty limits the capacity to adjust.

"It is not appropriate to call climate-induced disasters 'natural' and certainly not 'acts of God'. The use of the term 'natural disaster' can deflect attention away from the reasons for disasters -- the heavy use of fossil fuels by people in Western countries.

"A reduction in energy use by the biggest users, Western countries, is vital to reducing the impact of climate change on the poor. For individuals this means questioning lifestyles and use of energy, especially energy based on the use of fossil fuels. We need to recognise that our excessive use of fossil fuels is driving climate change and that the poor are bearing the brunt. From our government, we need coherent, consistent and ambitious policies to reduce carbon emissions.

"Unless action is taken, the poor could suffer more. Rising sea levels, shifting weather patterns and an increase in the frequency of extreme weather events -- these are killers. Vast areas of low-lying land could be inundated as glaciers and ice caps melt and sea levels rise. A half-metre rise in sea level would mean that land which now grows crops would become saline and barren. Climate change is not a distant threat but a present reality. A disease like malaria could spread into temperate regions, particularly those with high rainfall and good breeding conditions for mosquitoes.

"There is a storm coming. Millions of the poor are being made even poorer. The world must act now. No more excuses. We know what needs to be done. We have to change. All of us, from governments to individuals, all of us have a responsibility. How we play our role, how we exercise our responsibility, will determine the future of humankind. It will especially determine the lives of the poor." But when he arrived in Senegal, on that January day in 2007, little did David Fulshaw realise that he was heading into a storm of his own.

3

The law locks up the man or woman who steals the goose from the common. But the greater villain the law lets loose, who steals the common from the goose -- 17th century protest against English enclosure

Christmas 2006. Farna, her husband Musa and their children had attended the Christmas nativity play in the village church. When Joseph, with the pregnant Mary by his side, knocked at the door of the inn in Bethlehem, he was told "we have no room."

No room at the inn. The words stuck in Farna's throat. For her and her family there was no room on the land. There was no longer land that could sustain them, that could provide for them, that could grow enough food to keep them alive. There was only one thing left. They had to leave the village where she and Musa had been born, where their three children had been born. Well, five children in all. Two of their children had lived for less than a year. Those were dreadful days, those days when they died and were buried. Now, another dread was here. They had talked about this day. Some families in the village had already left for the capital city. where at least there was life.

The land had turned from green to brown, from soil to sand. Hardly a tree was left standing in and around her village. The villagers had cut them down for their own needs, and also to earn much needed money to supply townspeople with firewood. But with the trees gone, the soil had been left with no protection and the sand had spread. Crops cannot grow in sand, and the winds were getting stronger. Fierce winds hurled around the sand and often left it in large heaps. What if the sand buried us, wondered Farna at times. But it had already buried them, it had buried their livelihoods, their hopes. Life had changed beyond recognition. The wind even uprooted and swept trees away. The whole area had become a desert and was now full of sand dunes.

Land -- for them, there was no room on the land, there was no land they could use. What is land for? Farna asked herself. Land is for life, land is life, was her thought. But the land was effectively being taken from them. There was no longer any grass on their fields, no longer any living land in the village of their birth. They were being made to feel unwelcome in their own home.

Some years before, a London-based NGO had donated books to their village. Most were useful, although not all. One book that did not seem appropriate at the time had nonetheless stayed in Farna's mind. It was about a former British prime minister, Lloyd George. He was fighting against rich landowners in Britain and asked the question "Who made 10,000 people owners of the soil and the rest of us trespassers in the land of our birth?" Of humble Welsh origins, Lloyd George was said to be the only major politician in Britain who knew what it was like to be hungry, read Farna. And this had inspired him to work for the hungry.

"God gave the land to the people, the land," he had said, "The land, the land, the land on which we stand. Why should we be paupers with the ballot in our hand?" Today, Farna identified with those words. They had a vote, but she felt that a vote was of little use in their circumstances. She was being made to feel like a trespasser in the village of her birth, on their own special part of the planet. But who were today's equivalent of rich landowners, she wondered? God gave the land to the people, the land on which they stood. Farna could not believe that God would take land away from people. So how was it being taken away from them, she wanted to know.

Farna thought back to that conversation with the NGO worker who had told her about climate change, about how Western countries, with the United States the biggest culprit, were responsible for emitting greenhouse gases such as carbon dioxide that were causing the changing climate from which her family was suffering. And they were suffering. They were now worn out with hunger and thirst.

Suffering because wealthy nations far away were emitting all those gases. Wealthy nations were today's landowners, they were the villains beyond reach of the law. How could that be right?, she wondered. It was the big emitters of carbon who were effectively taking the land away from them.

The NGO worker had told her of something that a famous former United States president Abraham Lincoln had said: "The land, the earth God gave man for his home, sustenance, and support, should never be the possession of any man, corporation, society, or unfriendly government, any more than the air or water." Land, water, air. For Farna's family, only air remained. There was no workable land to possess.

It did not take Farna's family long to pack, they owned so little. Farna sensed that the children were crying silently as they mounted their few possessions on the back of their aging donkey. The donkey had helped take their crops to market in better times. But while his load was light, making progress was difficult. After four days of a journey, with little food and moisture and sleeping under what shelter they could find, they reached Senegal's capital city Dakar. They had become refugees in their own country. Sahel is Arabic for margin, Farna recalled, her family was now on the margin, of existence.

They made their way to the Cap Vert Peninsula area of the city where people from their village had already moved. The area was heaving. It had grown dramatically in recent years, due to people migrating from the rural areas. Hundreds of tiny and ramshackle sheet-metal shacks filled the narrow and litter-strewn streets, as well as tents and all shapes of canvass under which people lived.

Newcomers were not exactly welcome, the place had too many people already, but Musa managed to find someone who used to live in their village, and who helped them find a small area to stay. Farna, Musa and the children squatted with a canvas over their heads. It wasn't much, but now it was home. And there was a tap nearby., shared by hundreds of people like them.But it was a tap. Musa pounded the streets looking for work, anything. Farna tried to get the children enrolled in a school, but as they usually wanted payment this was difficult. They were slum dwellers, surviving on scraps from one day to the next, victims of climate change they had done nothing to cause. Hungry, destitute victims of other people who lived in another world.

4

Before setting off on his ride, David planned to spend two or three days in Dakar, getting used to the heat and humidity, and staying in a hotel near the city centre. It would be mainly a tent from then on. On his first day in Africa he lay by the hotel pool and did nothing. He reflected on how his travelling had changed him.

A few years beforehand, a visit to Jordan's Fertile Crescent had had a profound effect on him. Agriculture began on the Fertile Crescent -- an arc of land that sweeps through Palestine, Syria, Jordan, southeastern Turkey and western Iran.

For some 10,000 years, farmers along the Crescent had successfully grown cereal crops such as barley and wheat. There had been good years and not-so-good years but the Crescent had served them well. All the countries there could be classed as better-off developing countries, and this was largely because of the reasonably good land for agriculture.

But climate change had changed everything. There no longer enough rain to grow cereals. They had to replace cereal crops with olive trees which need less rain.

"Rainfall in this area seems to be less each year, we have seen a marked change over the last 30 years, and the land has become less productive," one farmer had told him. Like most farmers in the area he did not have irrigation and his crops were dependent on rainfall.

David wrote in an article for the Chronicle: "Part of Jordan's heritage is disappearing. It is disappearing because of climate change. The Fertile Crescent is no longer fertile -- rather it is now under serious threat. And it has happened so quickly. The crops that have grown for thousands of years have become unviable in just one generation.

"Farmers now have little option but to grow different crops, and many have been persuaded to grow olive trees. While they need less water, olive trees give them a lower return, and mean they have to buy more of their food.

"Farmers are replacing their wheat and barley with considerable reluctance. It takes five years after planting an olive tree to get a crop, and 10 years before the olives yield to their full potential. Hungry years lie ahead for these farmers and it is because of climate change."

His journeys had made him increasingly critical of United States policy on climate change. US policies he described as "an assault on the sovereignty of every other country in the world. We are, all of us, having US imperialism shoved down our throats. And the poor are being shoved out of existence."

His articles lambasted US selfishness and policy to the point where the US ambassador in London called to see the

Chronicle's editor to protest. But the editor stood by his reporter.

Western Europe was also a culprit, he was well aware of that, emitting more than its share of greenhouse gases but still only responsible for half the emissions per head of population, compared to the US.

David was ready to start turning pedals, but first wanted to see a little of Dakar. He wandered along the beach and watched small fishing boats bringing in their catch and selling it on the quayside. He spoke with a fisherman who told him that his catches had become so low that he could barely make a living. "The big trawlers," the fisherman had told him, "they catch fish that should be ours. Their boats are ruining our coastal grounds."

David turned inland and walked through Dakar's narrow streets, walked and walked for some distance. Until, and he had not planned it, he found himself in a shanty area. Ramshackle huts, some wood, some tin, tents and other canvas coverings were dominant.

"Please sir would you give me some money, I haven't eaten today," a small girl's pleading eyes gazed into his as she emerged from under a sheet of canvas.

"Stop that, you are not to beg," the child's mother bellowed, snatching her arm.

"I am sorry, she should not have troubled you. But we are very hungry. Forgive us," she said to David, her eyes down, not meeting his.

"It's ok, I understand," he said, offering some coins which were eagerly accepted with profuse thanks.

"We don't want to beg," she said, "I hate to see the children begging, to see what we've been reduced to."

"But tell me, how do you come to be here?" David instinctively asked. It was not too early to start understanding more about people's lives, he reasoned.

And Farna Gomis told him how the family had come to be there. She told the whole story of how life in her village had become impossible because of the changing climate. David insisted on making the family a contribution and went back to his hotel seething. "I have to do something with this. It can't wait," he told himself.

"Dan, I've got a good story," he blurted out, on getting through to the Chronicle's editor after several attempts.

"David, I cannot believe this. You have been in Africa for what, two days? You are supposed to be taking half a year off routine, and you have the gall to ring me so soon with a story. David, in those immortal words of a guy named Norman Tebbitt -- on your bike."

"Look Dan, you've got to listen, this family....," and David spilled it out. The gruff voice of the editor told him to e-mail it and said the paper would probably use it. "But I don't want to hear from you again until I'm eating my Easter egg," he warned in no uncertain terms.

So David Fulshaw wrote Farna and Musa's story, ending it by saying:

"The fact is that the way we live in the West is largely and directly responsible for the world's changing climate and the distress caused to people like Farna, Musa and their children. It is our heavy use of energy, in our vehicles, factories and homes, that causes emissions of greenhouse gases. And the United States is particularly culpable.

"To give people like Farna, Musa and their children a chance, to stop many thousands of others being driven like them from their villages in vulnerable areas, we must change the way we live. We must cut down on our use of energy. Not to do so would be the height of irresponsibility. The ball is in our court, it is especially in the court of the United States of America. It would be irresponsible for the US not to act to reduce its quite obscene level of carbon emissions."

In his Dakar hotel room David Fulshaw pressed the send button on his laptop and his story was on the news desk of the Daily Chronicle. And printed not only in the Chronicle, but also syndicated to papers around the world.

And he rang a contact of his, a producer on the Voice of America radio station. While most VOA output reflects the US voice, there were one or two radical programmes that were broadcast in the small hours of the morning when few were listening, where producers had more freedom, freedom to include items that were maybe critical of US government policy. David got through, the producer liked the idea of David sharing what he had seen in Dakar, and arranged to do a two-way interview on the phone, question and answer style.

He also rang Carol in London and told her what he was doing. Their relationship was over, but they remained on good terms. And Carol told him about a new man in her life, an American, a former climate change denier who used to work for the CIA before falling out with them for reasons he kept to himself.

The first day of cycling lay ahead, and the bed pulled hard. It was David's last day of luxury for a while. He took a swim in the hotel pool and just made it into breakfast before they started laying tables for lunch. The last person down for breakfast, he nonetheless took his time. David Fulshaw wanted to stoke up. Cycling can take a lot out of a rider. He would need more calories than normal.

He had brought energy bars and gels with him but they would not last long. Also a large packet of energy powder which poured into water should give him more energy. That too would run out, but he had arranged with the supplier to send him more when he asked. Difficult, as the supplier would have to send it to somewhere that David hoped to be in a week's time. In capital cities and large towns he may be able to buy something similar but he wasn't banking on it.

Water. He would need a lot. He planned to drink bottled when he could, but again was not banking on it. So he brought with him a large supply of water purification tablets. One small tablet would purify half a litre of water, the size of his drinking bottles.

The first three days of the journey would take him from Dakar to the town of Diourbel, some 160 kilometres to the east. He had been to Diourbel before and had a contact there who had invited him to stay overnight. The first day he planned to cycle only 40 km and then have two days of around 60 km. He wanted a start that would ease him in gently.

Senegal was a good starting point, a country with relatively good roads, fairly flat, although with rolling sandy plains not far out of the capital city. It was after midday when David wheeled his bike out of the hotel's grounds and pedalled slowly through Dakar's bustling streets. It was the worst time of the day to start, the hot sun beating down. At every traffic light where he stopped, someone tried to sell him something -- a belt for his trousers, a newspaper, a bar of soap, sunglasses, water.

The urban streets stretched out a long way, and the surface was poor at times. Potholes were the main hazard he needed to watch for. He tried to keep one eye down on the road and one eye looking ahead. Going down a bad pothole could throw him off or buckle a wheel.

Before reaching the open road he stopped for a drink from his bottle, a long drink. And readily bought a fill-up from a vendor who suddenly appeared.

The road east was busy and dusty, lorries belched out smoke and more than one skirted him by inches. Other than lorries, there were few cars but a lot of people, people walking everywhere, it seemed, often carrying heavy loads. David began to appreciate the joy of being back in Africa and the joy he now felt cycling. Africa was a great love of his, and so was cycling. Two joys together overwhelmed him, made him feel he had entered a very different world, a world of freedom. But he thought back to Farna and Musa. Where was freedom for them, he wondered, how long did they have to wait to be free of other people's lifestyles?

After a couple of hours, he pulled off the road, down what seemed a quiet gravel path, and ate a sandwich and some fruit that he had bought in Dakar. But within minutes a small group of children appeared and stood there wordless, watching him eat. It was a pattern that was to be repeated many times.

But the further he travelled the quieter the countryside became. Arid, and yet serene. Quiet and bustling with the beauty of nature. He was out on the road, uplifted by the cycling, by the rhythmic turning of the pedals. Bliss. Freedom. The constantly changing scenery meant that the road was never boring. Nuts, manioc and millet were all to be seen growing in the fields. But it was hot and the going was slow, and he stopped a lot to drink and to pause.

"You are welcome," a woman with a large basket on her head said to him, when he rode into a village at around five o'clock. With only an hour of daylight left, David decided that was enough for his first day.

He noticed a small bar by the roadside and went in for a beer. He talked with the bar owner, explained what he was doing and asked if he could pitch his tent for the night on ground at the back of the bar. The owner nodded and later in the evening served a local dish called Thiebou dieun -- fish, vegetables and flavoured rice. A satisfying meal that David was to eat a number of times in Senegal.

"Are you stopping in Thiès tomorrow, on your way east," the bar owner asked.

"No, I hadn't really planned that. Should I?" was David's response.

"I think you would find it interesting. Thiès is a kind of road and rail hub and has grown into something of a transit city where people from other parts of Senegal, and even from Mali, are coming almost every day. The city has become a refuge for street children. I know someone in Thiès who's a teacher and a voluntary worker with the street kids. I'll give you his address if you like. Remy Diop's his name. He would be happy to talk with you."

A heavily made-up woman of the night sauntered with swaying hips to where David was sitting near the bar, peered as closely as she could into his eyes and suggested that he buy her a drink. Unsuccessfully. This was a pattern to be repeated a number of times during his ride. He accepted the contact in Thiès with grateful thanks and went out the back to put up his instant-erect tent, which was true to its name, and to bed down for the night. His sleeping bag was thin and the ground was hard. He slept on and off till dawn, when he stumbled out to again experience the sheer beauty of an African sunrise.

Breakfast was bananas and once again rice. David packed up his tent and left soon after, wanting to get to Thiès, some 30 kilometres away, to hear more about the street children, why they were coming, what were their stories. He wanted to meet them and find out more. The road was good and the heat of the day lay ahead as he pedalled east, not entirely avoiding the inevitable potholes.

5

As he rode along on a day that was rapidly becoming hotter, David thought back ten years to a conference he covered in 1997 in the Japanese city of Kyoto. It was a conference that would put the name of Kyoto on the map. For in December 1997, a protocol of some significance was agreed.

'The Kyoto Protocol to the United Nations Framework Convention on Climate Change' laid down targets for the reduction of greenhouse gas emissions in countries that signed up -- 8 per cent reductions for the European Union, 7 per cent for the United States and 6 per cent for Japan. All by 2020.

The links between climate change and desertification were by then recognised. The Convention's preamble states that countries with "arid and semi-arid areas or areas liable to floods, drought and desertification" are "particularly vulnerable to the adverse effects of climate change." The Convention commits developed countries to cooperate in "the protection and rehabilitation of areas, particularly in Africa, affected by drought and desertification...."

But while the protocol was a step forward it was nowhere near enough to head off the threat of climate change. The

Intergovernmental Panel on Climate Change had estimated in 1990 that carbon dioxide emissions needed to be cut by 60 per cent. Although the Kyoto Protocol was proposing very modest cuts, even then the United States would not sign it. In the years following Kyoto, David Fulshaw had seen for himself some of the consequences.

After two hours of riding in the heat, David was on the outskirts of Thiès, holding the address of a school but with only a rough idea of how to get there. He rode through crowded, rutted streets to the city centre, jostled with clapped-out taxis, scooters, motorbikes and pedestrians, noticed a police compound and went in for instructions. Just behind the counter were thick steel bars fronting a sealed-off area. The faces of a dozen prisoners looked glumly and helplessly at him. But a policeman helpfully gave him directions to the school where he could find Monsieur Remy Diop.

The sound of children's voices could be heard several hundred metres away from the school. When he arrived at the gates he could see a large class being held outside. Children were sitting on the ground, a blackboard was perched against a tree, the teacher speaking in a local language.

David waited for a break which came not long after midday. The children, who started and finished school early, were soon scampering and yelling as they went home through the gates.

"Could you tell me where I could find Monsieur Diop?" he asked one of them.

"You go into the building and his room is on the right," was the reply.

Inside the school, it was mayhem with children emerging from their classrooms, running in all directions, teachers trying to keep order. There were no names on any doors but all the doors were open and eventually a curious child befriended him and took David to Monsieur Diop.

"Monsieur Diop," said David, as the two men held out their hands, "I'm David Fulshaw, an environmental journalist from the UK, and I was recommended to come and see you by someone you know who runs a bar, some 30 kilometres on the road to Dakar. I'm interested in the effects of climate change on people's lives and I gather that people, many children among them, who are affected by climate change, have come to Thiès. I wonder please if you could spare some time to talk with me?"

"Yes of course. Look, I am going home soon. Why don't you come and have some lunch with me?" It was an invitation gratefully accepted.

They walked through the busy streets to Remy Diop's home which was close to the Yakhine quarter of the city which he explained was the area where most of the street children lived. Over lunch he told David that in 1863 the French had built a fort at a village on the site of Thiès, and that commercial development soon followed, with the city becoming an important livestock-trading and meat-packing centre. Around a quarter of million people now lived there.

More recently it was children, some of them orphaned, who had flocked into Thiès, "many younger than ever, and growing in number," he said, "children who have no home other than the street. The Yakhine quarter, where most of them squat down, is the most deprived. We are trying to help. An orphans' association, mostly of teachers, has been set up to give treatment, help, nourishment, reading and writing lessons, and support. We have organised schools on the streets and in market areas, started training workshops for jobs, placed older children with craftsman under contract, organised dialogues with religious leaders, and also sporting activities. And we are trying to reunite them with the family when that is possible."

"Why have they become street children?" was David's question.

Some are orphans, some experience family break-ups, was the reply. Some came with their parents from villages north of here, driven out by a changing climate. But cramped conditions in the shanties meant there was no room for them in their parents' shack, so they left, and some had fallen under the influence of drugs, become violent and had broken their family ties.

"Something very disturbing has been happening in the last ten years or so," Remy Diop went on; "a growing number of the children who are coming here from the rural areas are what we call 'environmental orphans'. Land in their village has been devastated by low rainfall and a spreading desert. Their families cannot grow crops any more. In a bid to stay in their village, menfolk go to the towns and cities in search of work and in the hope of bringing some money back with them. Sometimes they return, but often the family never sees them again. With little food, there are tragic deaths. Sometimes mothers have come with their children and sometimes it is just the children. We have several children here who are in that position. Would you like to meet some of them?"

"Of course," replied David. The two men walked from the house down narrow bustling alleys to the Yakhine quarter of the city. Ragged children stared up at him, music blared noisily. But it was the smell rather than the sight of poverty that overwhelmed him. Poverty is so sanitised in the West, he mused, something that people read about, see on television, but which rarely touches their hearts. If people could smell it, they would be touched by it, he was sure.

Maria was eight years old and lived with her six-year old brother Mamadou on a pavement in the quarter. Their story was a hard one. They had lived in a village some 150 kilometres to the north. But their father left, they said, telling them that his land had become desert and could no longer grow crops. First of all their three-year old brother, then their one-year old sister had died. People said it was because they were malnourished. To make sure that her other children survived, their mother then began to divide the little food they had into two not three. The children insisted they she eat, but she said her taste buds had dried up and she no longer felt like eating. She fell ill and died.

Other people in the village looked after them for a while, but they had problems of their own and Maria and Mamadou said there was often no space or food for them. Finally they were turned out of where they were living. They hitched a lift on a lorry going to Thiès, somewhere they had heard that other children in their village had gone. They had since lived on the pavement in Yakhine. Environmental orphans. Maybe one day they would find their father, they said. They spent most of the day wandering around the city in the hope they would find him.

David looked at their forlorn faces and felt only helplessness and anger. Helpless to do anything very much, and anger that these young children had been reduced to this, victims of the irresponsibility of Western lifestyles, of governments, chiefly the United States, and their unwillingness to be serious about stopping the root cause of the children's problems, climate change.

"Can I give them some money, maybe pay for some accommodation for them?" David blurted out to Remy.

"I'd rather for now that you bought them some lunch and made a donation to the orphans association. If you give them money they would have no place to keep it and they could soon be robbed. There are a lot of desperate people round here. Your offer of paying for accommodation for them is a generous one, but I would rather you did it through the association. There are many unscrupulous landlords in this area. And we would prefer also to get them placed with a family," was Remy's response.

"The difficulty for us," he went on, "is that the children keep on coming. The orphans association is now enabling Maria and Mamadou to go to school on two days a week. But for children arriving today...tomorrow...what hope for them? I am worried that we will not be able to keep up. Africa will soon become a continent of refugees, a continent of orphans."

Two children among many. Innocent children who had done nothing to deserve their plight. David left them with a heavy heart, too moved and touched to say a word. When Remy offered him a bed for the night, his mood lifted and he gratefully accepted. But he struggled to make sense of what he had seen, and what he should do about it.

His mobile rang. It was Carol. "Alex, my partner, liked your story, and is warming to your views, but he said that you need to be careful. There's an outfit in the CIA called the Global Media Monitoring, Surveillance, Intelligence and Action unit, he says. Apparently it keeps tabs on everything that people are saying anywhere in the media about the US. They will have seen your story and will not like it one little bit. So do be careful."

Oh they are not going to bother with me, thought David, forget it. Over a meal that evening, Remy told him of the challenges that face African people at the best of times. "Every day, they struggle to survive. Almost half the people in Africa live in poverty, and we are the only region in the world where the number of people living in extreme poverty has almost doubled over the last two decades. By 2015, more than 400 million Africans could be living in extreme poverty. Climate change only serves to compound existing poverty by undermining water and food supplies, health, economic development and political and social stability. It's a really serious obstacle to development, and in some areas contributes to violent conflict."

"Their poverty leaves them so little leeway," he went on; "I am reminded of a visit that I made to the Eastern Cape province of South Africa just last year. After a long drive through rural areas, I stopped at a small shop to buy refreshments. Having chosen what I wanted, I went to the till to pay. Between me and the man behind the counter stood an elderly woman on

42

whose face was sculptured the narrative of poverty and suffering.

"The woman was carrying in one hand a loaf of bread and in the other a carton of milk. The man behind the counter rang the till and told her the price. Having pulled her piece of cloth from her chest, the woman untied its knot, opened it and laid it on the counter and began, in a tortuous manner, to count her coins, all copper. After completing the count, she painfully looked up at the man behind the counter. Staring straight into her eyes, with what appeared to be a standard emotionless answer, he told her: 'It's not enough, do you want the milk or do you want the bread?' That is some indication of what poverty is. It degrades, it kills, it's wrong, it should not go on.

"I gather that in Britain your athletes have a saying: 'pain is temporary, glory is eternal'. In the French language, 'pain' is our word for bread. And 'pain', bread, is too often only temporary for the poor, rather than something that's assured, and they see it as glorious if they survive to the end of another year. So we see your saying rather differently!

"Another factor about hunger is that it's seasonal for many peasant farmers," said Remy, "and climate change is making it worse. Let me explain. Farmers often grow enough food for about nine months of the year. They are fortunate if there is enough for the whole year. So they have three hungry months each year. But should the rains come late, or be lighter than usual, the harvest will be delayed or diminished and the hungry season will be longer, not three months but maybe four or five months. This is now happening all over Africa. In the hungry season, food on the market is scarce, prices soar, and food is beyond reach of the poor." He went on to speak of wider issues, of which he showed considerable awareness. His room was lined with books from floor to ceiling.

"This is just like my room back home," said David.

"Books are windows on the world, aren't they," said Remy. "A house without books is like a house without windows." A copy of "Time" magazine lay on Remy's shelves, the one with the famous cover 'Be worried, be very worried'. The climate is crashing, and global warming is to blame, it said. That cover opened the eyes of many people, The magazine pointed out that no one can say exactly what it looks like when a planet becomes ill, but it probably looks a lot like Earth right now, and that while global warming may be seen as a slow-motion emergency that would take decades to play out, few people appreciate that global climate systems are booby-trapped with tipping points and feedback loops, thresholds past which the slow creep of environmental decay gives way to sudden and self-perpetuating collapse.

"Specifically on Africa," Remy went on, "a recent report suggests that western and southern regions of Africa could warm by up to 10°C. Droughts will be more frequent and intense, particularly in sub-Saharan Africa, dry areas will become even drier, and there will be increased pressure on food-growing land. The rate of desertification has doubled since the 1970s, it said, with 12 million hectares of land lost to deserts every year. Meanwhile the earth's warming will lead to moisture loss and water scarcity in turn, and, as sea level rises, a substantial proportion of productive land along Africa's coasts will be lost." Facts like these hung heavily over David as he tossed in bed and tried to sleep on a hot, humid night.

6

Letter from climate. Imagine me as a person, a person by the name of climate. Think of me as global atmosphere if you wish. I have been around a long time, a very long time. Scientists date my age in line with the Big Bang theory of the origin of the Universe. It seems that conditions for this occurred around 13.3 billion to 13.9 billion years ago.

So I am no youngster. I have seen a few changes in my time. None more so than in the last two centuries. But let me take you back. I would like to give you a personal testimony.

I have varied in these 13 billion or so years. I have gone through glacial ages -- people on Earth like to call them ice ages. An 'ice age' is when continental ice sheets, polar ice sheets and alpine glaciers expand. My last major one was 22,000 years ago. And I have had warm periods too -- you like to call them "interglacials." But I have given you people on Earth reasonably calm weather over this time.

And you know something. Until about 200 years ago, my levels of carbon dioxide did not vary all that much. Why do I speak of carbon dioxide? Well, because it happens to be an important gas for me, and the level of it in my atmosphere matters a great deal to you. Let me explain.

In my last major glacial age the level of carbon dioxide in my atmosphere was around 180 to 200 parts-per-million CO_2 equivalent. That was over 22,000 years ago. It has risen slowly, very slowly, and in the year 1800 were 280 parts-per-million. In terms of the rise over 22,000 years -- 200 to 280 -- you could barely measure the annual increase.

But something huge then happened. Get ready for a shock. By 2000, only 200 years later, carbon dioxide in my atmosphere was 375 parts-per-million. That is a rise of nearly one part per million each year. And that is a frightening increase. It is unparalleled in my 13 billion years. If this goes on, then I will not be able to give you reasonably calm weather any longer. I, the climate, am changing, drastically. And you on Earth are causing me to change. I was created good, but what have you done to me?

Why have these changes happened? Because of the amount of industrial development in the last 200 years, especially a big increase in the use of fossil fuel energy. Carbon dioxide is a by-product of power stations, of buildings, factories and homes, and vehicles. And what are the consequences? Let's run through a few of them.

Your scientists are clever people. They can measure temperatures in the Arctic 650,000 years ago. Today's temperatures are the highest ever. In your 20th century, temperatures rose by just under one degree Celsius. If emissions of greenhouse gases continue to grow as projected, then average temperatures will increase by 2 degrees to 4 degrees Celsius in your 21st century. A rise of 2 degrees is dangerous for me -- and for you.

Look at the havoc that a rise of just under one degree in the last hundred years has caused. Your weather has become much more erratic, flooding has increased in severity and frequency, severe droughts have become more common, people are dying because of the changing climate and the poor are suffering the most. If a rise of one degree caused havoc, how much more disruption will a rise of 2 degrees cause to you humans? And I have to tell you that it is a self-induced rise.

It may not stop at a rise of 2 degrees. Your scientists are warning that a rise of 4 to 6 degrees may happen by the end of the century. Help! Both of us will be in big trouble. I will not be able to cope! You will not be able to cope. I will come back to that in a moment.

Another consequence is that with drought on the rise, the deserts are spreading, and people are being driven from their homes. The number of environmental refugees is now rising at an alarming rate. There could soon be 50 million. They are mostly people who live on the fringes of deserts who have seen the desert take over their land. People have abandoned their homelands with little hope of returning. And as many as 200 million people have been overtaken by disruptions of monsoon systems and other rainfall patterns, by droughts of unprecedented severity and duration, and by sea-level rise and coastal flooding.

And I have to tell you that weather systems will be driven by more energy as the temperature rises. That means rainfall will become fiercer and more erratic. It will be difficult for you to plan, because you will not know how the weather will turn out. A rise of 2 degrees by the end of the 21st century would mean that much less food could be produced. There would be a change in the boundaries between grassland, forest and shrub-land. This change in vegetation zones could cause famine in arid areas such as Africa.

Climate change could increase the number of hungry people by reducing the area of land available for farming. In many developing countries, the number of undernourished people could drastically increase. The severest impact could be in sub-Saharan Africa, where harvests could be down by a third. That means that a lot more people will go hungry.

And my lovely ice sheets in Greenland will start to melt. The Antarctic ice sheet will start to melt. When ice sheets from these two poles fall into the water, then the sea level rises. It also rises because water expands as it gets warmer. The sea level could rise by 60 centimetres. This would have a huge effect on your low lying areas of the world. It would make millions of people homeless and ruin valuable farmland.

In 2000, 46 million people lived in areas at risk of flooding. Your scientists believe that there could be a sea level rise of 60 centimetres in your 21st century and that a rise of that kind would increase the number of people at risk to 90 million. Worst hit would be Bangladesh, Vietnam, island states and the low lying area of the Nile Delta. Eventually it would also be coastal cities such as New York, Tokyo, Hong Kong, Calcutta, Karachi -- and also London. And there would be more disease. Again it is happening already. According to your World Health Organization 150,000 people are already dying every year from climate change, due to an increase in diseases. *(to be continued).*

7

Diourbel lay some hundred km to the east of Thiès, a day and a half of cycling on David's schedule. Remy left for school early and it suited David to make an early start with the aim of covering most of the distance that day.

Cycling just before eight, the day was already hot, the events of yesterday, the encounter with Maria and Mamadou, swirling through his mind. He was out here enjoying himself, while they were battling for survival in a city that was previously just another name, a name barely on his itinerary. But now it was a city that for him had become much more, a place where life for many people hung in a precarious balance, where orphaned children were reduced to sleeping on the streets.

The city's roads dragged on, the air full of exhaust fumes and dust, roadside traders offering a vast array of goods. Eventually David took a deep breath as he reached an undulating open road, not a bad surface either. As he pedalled through the first village of the day, a slim young woman emerged from a mud hut, elegantly dressed and walking beautifully. Looking, it seemed to David, as though she was on the cat-walk of a fashion show. It was just one of the many surprises he was to encounter.

With every kilometre he pedaled the temperature was rising, until the cycling became uncomfortable. At around noon he decided to stop for a break, a long break in an isolated spot. A large tree by the roadside offered him shade and sanctuary. He unfolded bread he had bought in Thiès, also some cheese, and although he had thought he was a long way from anywhere, a small group of children came up to look at him.

A girl of about ten said a quiet "Bonjour Monsieur," otherwise no words were exchanged. Why were these children, most of them girls, here and not at school, wondered David. But then he remembered that many girls in Africa are lucky if they go to school, even primary school. Again he pondered on what he was doing, about the whole rationale of cycling through Africa like this, a dot of affluence among children suffering an injustice.

Thoughts like this made his lunch as uncomfortable as cycling in the heat. But the children eventually wandered off and David dozed under the shade of the tree. And dozed and dozed.

He thought back to an experience which had had a profound effect on him, a visit to Ethiopia, just two years beforehand. In one area of Ethiopia, farmers had told him that they used to get two rainy seasons a year, a long and a short one. But the short season rains had completely disappeared, they said, and they were too poor to afford irrigation.

Without rain, there were no crops. That meant hoping to harvest enough in September to last for 12 months. And that was almost impossible. There were several hungry months of the year which some people did not survive. Climate change had again changed everything.

He recalled a visit to Peru where there was a different kind of problem -- cold, freezing cold weather, which was again related to climate change. Temperatures in the winter months were becoming lower and lower, plunging to below zero for long periods. Many people, especially the poor in highland areas of the country, were not strong enough to cope with the sub-zero conditions. Children, women and men were dying, animals were dying. For many thousands of people, life was totally disrupted.

He also remembered a visit to the USA to spend a week with a colleague at his home in the suburb of a major city, and being shocked by what he witnessed. Families were entirely dependent on their cars. Everyone old enough to drive had a car. And they would get into their cars to make a journey of 100 metres down the road. The concept of walking, of cycling, had gone. Cycle lanes, even sidewalk pavements, did not exist. Public transport was almost non-existent. Gasoline was dirt-cheap. The scene he witnessed was one of suburban selfishness, without any thought for the impact on people elsewhere in the world.

David's lunch-time slumber was rudely interrupted by the eyes of a skinny dog inches away from his own. The dog had been like the children -- silent. Until, that is, David's startled cry sent the dog barking and yapping fiercely around him. This dog could have rabies, was his first thought, his second to grab for the bike pump and fend it off. Eventually, to his immense relief, the animal got the message and wandered away. And

David made a mental note that it would be best not to doze off in the open.

The post-lunch road was good, although extremely busy at times. He struggled to stay upright after failing to spot a large pothole. Frequent stops for water were again needed and the going was slow. Cycling into a village as the sun was just about to go down, he decided to call it a day. A ramshackle looking bar stood back from the road. The door almost came off in David's hand as he opened it. A few dusty looking cans of soft drinks and the odd bottle of beer dotted the bar's only shelf. No sign of life. No sign of food, and he was seriously hungry, cycling being notable for burning up calories.

He sat down on an ancient bench and nibbled on his emergency nuts. Eventually a rather surly woman appeared from behind the bar. To David's dismay she shook her head when asked if food was served. No food here, no food anywhere in this village, was her message.

He thought of going on but it was now almost dark and cycling on could have been risky. The woman gave permission for him to pitch his tent at the back, a modest charge was negotiated, and he prepared to settle down for the night.

Hunger. Economists have a theory that nowhere in the world does anyone go hungry who has money in their pockets. In a small village in Senegal, the theory was that evening about to be proved wrong. David had money in his pocket but was hungry, just for one night joining the 800 million in the world who go to bed hungry every night. So he thought. But as he lay there on the lumpy ground, music on his iPod helping him to forget the hunger pains, he heard the woman outside the tent calling "monsieur, monsieur, we are about to eat. You are welcome to join us."

It was an invitation that monsieur accepted with gratitude. He accompanied the woman into a small room behind the bar, a room with no table or chairs, with a man and five children, aged from about 5 to 15, sitting on the floor, with a bowl of rice on a mat in the middle. Also some tomatoes and green peppers.

A chair from the bar was offered to David but sitting on it made him feel self-conscious and after a minute he opted for the floor. While everyone else put their fingers in the rice and scooped it out, David was given a fork. Not a word was spoken as they ate. When the bowl was empty, and it did not take long to empty, the children moved off, the man stood up and silently shook hands with David. Refusing payment, he bid him "Bon soir." David pulled a packet of soft mints from his pocket and asked if he could give them to the children.

Back in the tent, David picked up squeals of laughter from the children. He hoped it was because of the mints. Grateful for the experience of eating with the family, grateful for the food, he was nonetheless soon hungry again.

Sleeping badly, he was also suffering from insect bites, and they were becoming painful. "The occurrence of mosquito and other insect bites can be minimised by wearing long-sleeved shirts, long pants and hats to reduce exposed skin," he had read somewhere. But this advice was impractical to useless. When the temperature was over 30 degrees Celsius, who wants to wear long clothing, he wondered.

He had applied repellents to his clothing, shoes and tent, and carried a lightweight mosquito net. He just hoped the mozzies would get to know that. Keeping his mind on other things, decided David, was the best way to forget about the bites. He resolved to be off at first light, when he would ride into Diourbel, now only 30 km away.

He looked at a report he was carrying. Poverty in the sub-Saharan Africa region was closely linked to the region's environmental degradation, he read. Since the beginning of independent Africa in 1960, the region had been subject to a widespread depletion of agricultural and natural land areas, exploitation of resources and a serious decline in water quality.

The injustice was stark. Africa has the world's lowest carbon emission rates. Africans were bearing the brunt of other people's emissions. And those who had contributed least to the atmospheric build-up of greenhouse gases were also the least equipped to deal with the negative impacts.

"Wealthier nations that have historically contributed and are continuing to contribute the most to global warming through unsustainable consumption and production patterns are better able to adapt to the impacts," he read. "The tragedy of climate change is the fact that whereas the north bears the largest responsibility for the causes of climate change, the south and especially Africa are the most vulnerable to the worst consequences of climate change."

A growing number of people had become environmental refugees, driven from their homes because the environment was damaged and useless for life, it said. They were classed as "Internally displaced persons," a phrase that only served to sanitise their dire predicament, thought David. Beneath that high-sounding phrase lies heartbreak. The people were exiles in their own land. "Environmentally induced migrants" was another, much better phrase that was also used.

"Climate canaries" was also a phrase used to describe people displaced by climate change. Described in that way, because the phrase could be taken to mean people who had flown from a local climate that could not sustain them. Again it could refer to change that might be a warning that something far more significant and environmentally damaging was not far away. Whatever they were called, the people who had been driven from their land by climate change received none of the support that was given to refugees.

Under the Geneva Convention the international community is obliged to protect and assist refugees with shelter, food and medical help. But not so internally displaced persons. Although they were refugees from the land, they were left to fend for themselves, the forgotten victims of someone else's lifestyles.

These displaced persons were not only finding their way to already overcrowded cities or environmentally fragile areas of neighbouring countries, but the situation was dramatically worsening. There were now estimated to be almost 20 million internally displaced persons, half of them in Africa. That was in 2006. But researchers estimated that the number of environmental refugees could increase more than sevenfold, to 150 million by 2050. The Red Cross was saying that more people are now displaced by environmental factors than by war.

From 20 million people to 150 million people in little more than 50 years, this was the stark possibility. And every one of them was a individual, struggling to live.

Hungry he may have been the next morning, bitten David certainly was, but the incomparable African dawn struck him as more beautiful than ever. He wondered if being empty of food meant that he had more room inside him to appreciate other gifts, like the gift of Africa's morning light. He dismissed such a romantic notion and, in the first village he rode into, found a cafe that served the traditional dish of fish and rice.

Diourbel stands at a geographical crossroads, the Sahel and the desert lay to the north, while more fertile land lay in the south. David had visited the city some three years ago and remembered that it had an Internet cafe. So he decided first to check his e-mails. After over a week, there were hundreds, mostly rubbish. But there were some reactions also to his piece from Senegal, mostly favourable, while a few accused him of anti-Americanism.

An agriculturalist that David met on his previous visit to Diourbel had kept in touch and offered him accommodation if he ever came back. Andre Sylla lived in a relatively spacious house on the outskirts of the city that took some finding. Guard dogs yapped menacingly at the cyclist as he dismounted in front of the tall gates that guarded the property. Andre greeted him, calmed the dogs and the men went inside.

"Since you were last here, what was it, three years ago," said Andre, "things in the villages north of here in the Sahel have become much worse. Whole villages are being abandoned, more and more of them, and people are flooding down here, to towns in the south, some going to Côte d'Ivoire. The immediate reason is not enough rain to water their crops and livestock. The deeper reason is climate change, which of course these villagers have done nothing to cause.

"The villagers do not call it climate change. Rather they speak of changes in the weather, or changes in weather patterns. Call it by any name you like, these people are innocent. The guilty are United States policy makers who refuse to do anything to limit their carbon emissions. There's a disaster unfolding, David, you know that but I doubt if you know how bad it is. Spend a couple of days with me and I'll show you. But before we go anywhere I'd like you to read some stories from people living in the Sahel who are affected."

The stories told of what was happening. "In the past, the bush was full of trees and the harvest was good," said a 72-year old man. "Grasses flourished. There was geese and game, a lot of wild animals, panthers, hyenas, hares and deer. I have seen them with my own eyes. In the river there were crocodiles and hippopotami. There used to be hunters in our village, but now there is no more game.

"There was no sand in the river before. The river has been getting shallower and shallower for some time now because it doesn't rain any more. When I was young, boats from St Louis passed by on their way to Kayes in Mali. People came by canoe, bringing salt, pepper and other spices which we used to buy. In the past, the wind was strong but there wasn't the dust there is today. During the cold weather, the rain fell in bucket-loads. Now it no longer pours as hard during the rainy season. I have lived through seven years of drought."

A 63-year old woman wrote: "Before, when there was plenty of rain, the waters came up to the village and we could live off fish. Now the waters don't rise any more and the river has become shallower. All the villagers went fishing together with the permission of the village chief. There were so many fish that we would dry some to eat during the winter.

"It used to be that the rains always came. Since the rains have stopped the young can no longer produce good harvests. That is why they have emigrated. There is nobody left in the village."

And a 69 year old woman said: "Things are more difficult since the rains no longer fall. We used to harvest 10 to 15 bags of maize and sweet potatoes. Today they can never gather more than three bags. There used to be a clear demarcation between the seasons. The climate was a kind one. It enabled us to reap large rewards from small areas of cultivation. Nowadays, we can sow our seeds and still not reap any harvest."

"The climate was a kind one." David reflected on those words. But look at it now.

"Yes, and there's more you can read later. But come and see for yourself now. Let's drive north," said Andre.

8

The car headed through the packed streets and along a main road for several miles before taking a track into the bush. It was flimsy bush, the thin trees spaced out rather than packed together. After bumping along for some miles, Andre stopped the car and beckoned David to come with him. The two stood on land where there was nothing.

"There used to be a village here," said Andre, "a village where over a thousand people lived. Now there is nothing, not a stick left, nothing but a disused well and neem trees. People could no longer survive here. Those neem trees -- the village was originally built around those trees. They're great trees, virtually every part of them is useful. They have seeds and oil, as well as bark and wood. The villagers left some years ago and took everything with them, or came back later for them -- their houses, everything. Nothing was wasted. Their poverty meant that every scrap of metal, of wood, whatever, had to go with them."

There was a silent ghostliness about the place that chilled David's spine. The ghost of a village past. The ghost of an impersonal but devil-like changing climate that had driven people out. They drove on silently some 20 kilometres through parched landscape to another village. Here there was life. Andre knocked at the door of the village headman. After the usual greeting and offering of drinks, the headman talked about the problems the village faced.

"Until recently about 400 people lived here. Over a hundred have now left. The problem is water. Gradually lower rainfall, over the last ten years, especially, has left us with not enough rain for crops or livestock. There is not enough food, not enough water for people to drink. Are you aware that in some African languages the word for water is the same as the word for life? No water, no life. I am really fearful for our future."

As the three of them sat and talked in that parched village, the injustice of what was happening to these people hit David like never before. The injustice of it was combined with a feeling of powerlessness to do any anything about it. He could write about it, but would anyone take any notice, he wondered. Did anyone in authority care enough? After saying their au revoirs, they drove on to another village. One that seemed larger but eerily emptier. Again the village headman was their first call. But the response was cool. Conversation was hard going.

"It has been a difficult day for me," the headman finally said. "There has been a steady stream of people leaving the village because of the way our climate is changing. But today my own brother and his family are leaving. I have done all that I can to get them to stay, but to no avail. Come with me and meet them."

They walked along a long dusty path to the house of a family loading a donkey cart with their possessions. The headman explained who the visitors were, but few words were spoken. David found he could barely look at what was happening, a scene he realised that was probably being repeated every day in homes throughout the Sahel region of Africa. People turned into refugees in their own country.

"Have you come far?" asked the village headman's brother looking at the car. On hearing they had come from Diourbel, the man went on: "You may think we are simple people but we listen to the radio and we hear that cars are polluting the atmosphere and contributing to changes in weather patterns, including lack of rain. It's this that is driving us from our homes." It was all said in a matter-of-fact voice as he continued to load the cart. David felt about as small as a beetle that was threading its way along the ground. "I promise you," he said, "I am trying to do something about it. I just ask for your forgiveness for the way we live."

Little more was said, the heartache of the moment was apparent for everyone. The men drove back to Diourbel, talking little but with David thinking much. Eventually breaking the silence, he said: "I felt so awful back in that village, so powerless, those people, innocent victims of the way we live in the West, victims of the policies of governments, especially the USA. What can I do, Andre? Can I cycle round Africa while this is going on?"

"David, you are a journalist, you are sitting on a barrel of ink. Use it. Tell the world what you have seen David, tell the world, that's what you can do."

"Yes, I'd like to do it straightaway, but I'm supposed to be taking half a year off routine work. I've already sent one story. My editor's going to kill me if I ring him again now."

"But today you have had first hand experience of what is happening and maybe you should write it down while it's still fresh in your mind. And you have not finished here yet. Tomorrow I'd like you to meet some of the environmental refugees who have come here. The UN calls them internally displaced persons, but that's a sanitised term. They are refugees. Refugees in their own country, victims of other countries."

And the following day he did meet some of them. Whole families of environmental refugees living on pavements, on railway tracks, in improvised tents made of plastic sheets and discarded bamboo, desperately trying to survive. Andre introduced David to a man and a woman who had arrived in the camp some two years ago. They earned a meagre living selling goods at the roadside to passing vehicles and pedestrians.

"We're not able to save enough money to move on," said the man, "we're trapped. Returning home is our dream, but somehow I doubt if we ever will."

"Environmental refugees have lost everything," Andre told David. "They don't have the money to move. We do what we can, but no agency is helping them with funds to allow them to move on. Environmental refugees are not recognised in world conventions." Nearly everyone that David spoke with told him of a member of their family who had not survived their forced migration. One woman sobbed as she told of the death of her three-year-old daughter. "What had she done to deserve that," she managed through the tears.

"Climate change is a killer," he said to Andre later, "a killer and a thief. Its consequences are killing people and robbing them of their livelihoods, their homes. The policies that cause it...are a crime...a crime against humanity."

"Don't tell me David, I say again, tell the world. And keep on telling it. One day the world will listen."

"I've got to wait for a week or two but yes, of course I will write. But I think I'll wait till I get further along, maybe to Mali, to Bamako. By then I expect I will have seen even more."

"Well, you have about 500 kilometres more to go just to the Mali border. You're not going to cycle all of it are you?"

"I'd like to, but I've got a bag for my bike. If the going gets rough I'll catch a bus."

"I'd advise you not to. The buses between here and Mali are dilapidated and frequently break down. They are also very over-crowded. You could have real problems with your bike. Even in a bag, the driver may want you to put it on top, outside, and it could be damaged or even stolen. There is a railway that runs to Mali. I suggest that when you eventually ride into Tambacounda, that's about two-thirds of the way to the Mali border, just over 300 kilometres from here, you take the train to Mali." To David, it sounded good advice.

The road to Tambacounda went through semi-desert country but the road, while bumpy at times, was mostly good. David managed the 300 km east in four days pedaling and sleeping overnight in his tent. While the wind and the sand seemed to blow at him from all directions, they were relatively uneventful days, apart from a chance meeting that left him hopping mad.

On the third day of the journey on a quiet stretch of road with sand blasting in his face, he noticed a family trudging along the sand on a path from the north. Two adults and three ragged children were slowly pushing a handcart and seemed close to exhaustion. A young girl was sobbing. "I am so thirsty," David heard her say. He stopped and offered his water bottle. The eyes of the girl, of the whole family, lit up, and his entire supply of water was downed in minutes.

He asked them about their journey. The family's story was by now all too familiar. They were leaving their village in the Sahel because they could no longer survive there. Their ancestors had lived in the village for centuries. But the rain had gone, their crops had withered, their livestock had died. Food was short, the wells were drying up, they were hungry, the children malnourished, thirsty beyond endurance. Then the blow fell. Their youngest child died from malnutrition at only four months old. The woman tearfully pulled a picture of the child out of her bag to show David, a picture that had been taken by a visitor. And David wept with her.

"We fear hunger, we really fear it," said the woman, "we fear dying of hunger. No one knows what hunger is like unless you've suffered from it. Hunger reaches deep into your bones, makes you feel dizzy, it's a fire in your stomach that only goes out when you eat. But what must it be like when you don't eat, day after day, and in the end it kills you. That's why we are fearful. I dread to think what my child suffered."

The woman pulled out a scrap of paper, which had a prayer on it. The prayer was headed "Give me bread." It read: "Give me bread, let it be burnt or stale, it kills the fire in my stomach…In exchange, take whatever you like. I could surrender the freedom of my country for bread. Love, sadness, thought, I set at nothing. I would give all for bread."

Their child's death was the end for the family, said the woman. They decided to go. The problem was they had nowhere to go, no money, nothing. Anger, sheer anger, was David's overriding emotion. He asked if he could give them some money, it was the only thing he could do. They accepted with profuse thanks. And as they trundled off, he decided to write something in Tambacounda, and make it stronger than ever.

Tambacounda used to be part of Mali, David had read, and was famous for its drums and dance culture. In the late afternoon, when he rode into the centre, it was bustling with people, traffic and noise. He decided to forsake his tent and spend two nights in a hotel, somewhere with e-mail facilities, where he could write and relax. He needed to write, he needed to rest.

He e-mailed his editor, making no apologies. "Dan, I know you told me not to make a habit of this, but what I've seen, the people I've talked with, they've given me new insights into what climate change is doing to African people. I'd like to write something right now, while it's still fresh in my mind." The editor's reply, on the lines: "I might had known I hadn't seen the back of you for six months," gave him the go-ahead. And that was the pattern for the months ahead. David told the story from the human angle, told of the people he had met in Thiès, in the villages north of Diourbel, and on the road to Tambacounda. Global warming, climate change was the root cause of their problems, he said, and ended:

"A deep human tragedy is unfolding here in West Africa. I have seen for myself the criminal devastation of the environment, devastation that is destroying people's lives and homes. The Africans I met have nothing, have done nothing to cause it. They need funds to help them re-settle, but above all, policies from big carbon-emitting countries to reduce their carbon emissions and tackle climate change in a serious manner.

"While the people I met have contributed nothing to global warming, they are dying from its effects. George W Bush, in particular, is displacing and killing untold thousands of people through irresponsible policies on climate change. Bush will not sign the Kyoto Treaty because he's in hock to the polluting oil, gas and mining interests that back him. Bush talks of tackling climate change by investing in new technologies. The fact is that the USA is investing only pitiful amounts in such technologies.

"Bush talks of democracy, but his policies are invading people's sovereignty. He talks of defeating terrorism, while doing nothing to stop climate change. And this is a far greater threat to life than terrorism. Why does the US fail to recognise this? Because of the selfish pursuit of money. Bush is a disgrace to humankind. International law should change so that he can be prosecuted for manslaughter. And it should be changed so that victims can claim damages from those who cause the problem."

He concluded by saying: "George W Bush has a strong claim to be the world's most irresponsible leader and the United States the world's most irresponsible country. I suggest that every reader sends them a parcel of sackcloth and ashes to allow them to repent -- and above all to change their policies and stop the tragedy." He punched the Send button, and again rang his Voice of America contact, and did an interview down the line.

9

Mali. It was almost the end of January, a month into his journey, and it hit David that he was still in one country. He had to get out of Senegal and into Mali soon, he thought, and decided to take the train to the Mali border.

David had visited Mali before, just two years before, and had with him a copy of the feature he had then written for the paper:

"Noisily and incessantly the sand swirled around as a nine-year-old girl pounded millet into flour. She joked with a villager and smiles lit up their faces, smiles of happiness that hid misfortune. The 800 people of this village in eastern Mali were facing starvation after one of the worst droughts in living memory, a drought which devastated food output.

"Whereas the villagers normally harvest around 600 kilos a hectare of their staple food, millet, last October -- six months ago -- they harvested only 30 kilos. 'On most of our fields we had little more than stalks,' a villager told me.

"I looked at fields that resembled a dust bowl. The people have little food in their barns and little money to buy food from outside the village. There will not be another harvest until

October this year. The villagers see little chance of outside help; they told me that last year they received a kilo of cereal for the whole village.

"A growing number of the villagers are leaving in search of work, food and money to bring back to the village to help them survive. It's a desperately precarious existence; people may be forced to abandon their homes and villages altogether and add to the growing number of environmental refugees.

"Along semi-desert roads in this part of Africa I came across village after village where illiteracy is almost total. What is the answer for the 9 year-old girl with a lovely smile, I wondered, and for the many children like her? I felt frustrated and powerless about being able to do so little to help. And yet I can help. For I am part of an energy-guzzling society which is causing the climate to change. I can help, we can all help to end what is surely a scandal."

Now he was going back to Mali. His immediate difficulty was that only one express train a week ran north from Tambacounda to Kidira on the Senegal-Mali border and it departed, or was due to depart, at the unearthly hour of 3.25 in the morning. In bed by 9.00 the night before, having first gone through a time-consuming process of buying a ticket and reserving a seat, David was ready to get up at 3.00 a.m. for a scramble to the station. But the train was coming from Dakar and was frequently late, he had been told. The hotel night porter said he would try to find out what time it had left Diourbel and ring him. At 3.00 a.m. he rang; the train was two hours late. A 5.00 a.m. start was not that bad.

He counted himself lucky that there was a train. Only a few years earlier, in 2003, the Dakar to Bamako service had been suspended because of the condition of the track. A Canadian company was now operating the service, but the carriages were reported to be poor, "due to be updated soon," said the company.

Certainly needed it, thought David, as he squashed himself into a narrow seat on the crowded train. While it made frequent unscheduled stops, the train managed to roll into the Senegalese-Mali border town of Kidira just after noon. David's bike in the bag was a bulky nuisance but survived.

He got off the train, hot, dusty and hungry, reassembled his bike and faced customs. Two lots of customs, one to leave Senegal, one to enter Mali. A Senegalese border guard carefully and laboriously scrutinised his passport and visa, and asked questions about his bike. Finally, the necessary leaving stamp was hammered onto his passport. He said goodbye to Senegal, cycled over the border to the town of Diboli in Mali to face customs again. His visa for Mali was in order but the customs official nonetheless demanded payment of 5 euros. Extortion, a bribe, but David decided to pay it rather than risk being held there for hours.

Mali was listed in a United Nations report in 2003 as the fourth least livable country in the world. Certainty one of the world's poorest countries, in terms of income, life expectancy and literacy rates.

Cycling again after a few days out of the saddle, David soon felt tired in the baking heat. After a hour in a wayside bar, he got the pedals turning at a steady enough speed, although it was by then almost mid-afternoon. Bamako, the capital city, was his next big stop but that lay over 600 kilometres away. The train he had just got off ran close to the route he was taking, and was his reserve option. The first centre of any note was Kayes, some 100 kilometres from the border he had just crossed. He wanted to reach there the following day.

The road was not as good as most of the roads David had used in Senegal. He bumped along slowly through dusty savannah country until it was almost dusk. Coming into a small village with small wooden shacks, he noticed a faded 'Bar' sign over a door. After a drink or two, he enquired about food, and, some considerable time later, was handed a plate of something which would normally have been in the uneatable category, but he needed to take on energy.

He pitched his tent on rough ground behind the bar and collapsed into his sleeping bag, tired out after his early start. While he slept well at first, he woke up, freezing cold in the small hours of the morning. Hot days, freezing nights he had experienced in Senegal, but this time he had more difficulty than ever keeping out the bitter cold.

He packed up and left the village just after dawn to get the best of the day for his ride to his next stop, the city of Kayes. He was now deep in the harsh semi-desert of the Sahel. It was hot, dry, dusty and felt remote, with the road often stretching endlessly ahead. The monotony was broken only by the occasional river that meandered through the parched landscape.

But the monotony was soon to be broken in a way that no cyclist would want. On a quiet stretch of road, David struggled up a long hill and as he slowly reached near the top, a large thick-set man was standing in the middle of the road. As David approached him, the man pulled out a large knife, thrust it menacingly to within inches of David's chest and grunted: "Give me your wallet."

While David's heart sank, he was aware that this kind of attempted robbery might happen somewhere on the journey, and had taken the precaution of carrying two wallets. The main one was tucked away deep in his panniers, while the other one, a "mock wallet" in his pocket, normally carried just a few small domination notes. As David pulled out the mock wallet, there was only a 5 euro note in it.

"I'm travelling light," said David lamely.

"What! Well if this is all you have, I will take the bike instead," said the man. David instinctively moved his bike between him and the robber. As the man tried to grab the bike with both hands, he dropped the knife and when he bent to pick it up, David seized his chance. Mounting the bike quicker than he had ever done before, and already in a low gear through going uphill, he pedalled furiously over the brow of the hill. In hot pursuit, the robber threw himself at David's back wheel but missed and fell spreadeagled to the ground. David was away, going fast downhill towards Kayes, and thanking his lucky stars.

The region around Kayes is often described as "the pressure cooker of Africa" due to its extreme heat. David sweated through villages of circular thatched huts and crumbling buildings, past the occasional farmer who stopped, gazed and sometimes waved as he rode past.

Kayes seemed to him a dusty place in the middle of nowhere. A city of some 100,000 inhabitants, at least it afforded some amenities. Stopping outside a police station which seemed to have spacious grounds, he asked if he could pitch his tent in their compound for the night and this was agreed. Staying in a police compound was a tip he had picked up from an African cyclist. But he had a limited choice of places to eat. A meal of chicken, rice, beans and tomatoes, washed down with a couple of indifferent local beers, left him feeling vaguely unwell.

Leaving Kayes David was faced with a headwind, strong enough to make his progress very slow. He was also on roads that deteriorated into little more than dirt tracks. The inevitable happened. Only a few miles out of town he heard the dreaded hissing noise from his back tyre, his first puncture of the journey. He had decided not to mend punctures by the roadside, but rather just to replace the inner tube and do the repair later in the day. But changing the tube was messy and left his hands oily. He rode on towards Bamako, some 500 km away. At 80km a day he hoped to make it in six days. He knew that a daily train service ran between Kayes and Bamako, but hoped he wouldn't weaken.

He weakened. But not until the third day after mile upon mile of the same kind of dusty country and with the wind showing no sign of easing. The sight of a railway station close by the road was too much, especially as the timetable said a train was due in just over an hour. He waited. The train came in after three hours and arrived in Bamako late at night. No place for a tent, he thought, and crashed out into a B&B near the station.
The bustling city of Bamako nonetheless came as a relief to David after his days in the Sahel. Bamako is estimated to be the fastest growing city in Africa, one of the largest in West Africa.

The film "Bamako" had been made the year before. The film depicted two sides of the argument over whether the World Bank and IMF, or corruption, are guilty of the current financial state of many poverty-stricken African countries.

The day after arriving, David wandered through streets packed with people, cars, motorcycles, mopeds, donkey carts, hand carts, vans, taxis and bicycles, with the pavements full of vendors. Tiny stalls offered a vast range of goods, but bored-looking vendors seemed to have few takers. The air was also full of dust and exhaust fumes, with the smallest vehicles, the mopeds, seeming to be the biggest polluters.

Every time he stopped for a moment, someone would come up and start a conversation. He passed small huts with people crammed together sleeping on floors or thin mattresses. He went into the office of an aid agency and was told that environmental refugees were coming to Bamako in increasing numbers. The agency had organised 'Change of address' cards for the displaced to send to President Bush. These had a picture of a family trudging from a barren landscape, with the words 'Change of address' underneath. Inside the card read:

"We are changing our address from a village in northern Mali, where our ancestors have lived for centuries, to a pavement further south. We did not want to move, but we cannot survive in our village any longer. We wanted you to be the first to know. And we want to say that you can do something to restore hope to millions of people in Africa whose lives and homes are threatened. Threatened by changes in weather patterns, by your carbon emissions. Reduce them. Please. Yours from an African sidewalk...."

10

Washington D.C. Today was the first day of his new diet. As 41-year old Tom Glickmann padded his 24 stone along the corridor of a plush federal office block in Washington D.C. he told himself that he was going to be a good boy and keep to the diet. Well, as close as he could anyway. He needed to lose weight, his wife, his doctor, and the few leaner friends that he had were telling him.

But as he swung open the door of the office, he took comfort from the fact that his same-age colleague Bruce Fieldon was only a stone or two lighter.

"First day of my new diet today, Brucie," he announced, "sales of doughnuts, fresh whipped cream cakes and cookies are going to slump."

"That's a pity, Tom, because I've just come back from the canteen and wow you should see their new delivery of cakes. The most mouth-watering things I've ever seen, and the aromas, aromas to die for. I've sampled a few already, I can tell you."

"Get thee behind me Satan," was the brisk if half-hearted response.

"Yeah, but I'm sure the cakes taste lovely when they hit the back of your mouth."

"I'll ignore that. So what's cooking today Brucie -- work, that is, not food you fool."

"Global Media Monitoring, Surveillance, Intelligence and Action unit" read the sign on their door. Part of the CIA, the unit monitored and surveyed what was going on in the world, going on anywhere in the media, that had any connection whatsoever with the United States of America. Nobody in the media was doing anything, anywhere, saying, writing, broadcasting anything about the USA that the unit did not know about. And if Tom, Bruce and his colleagues did not like it, if they did not like what was being said, they acted. Free speech of course they believed in, provided naturally that people spoke in a responsible way. Nobody, nowhere got away with anything that besmirched the good name of the United States of America. Federal orders at the highest level were their authority.

"Most of it's pretty tame stuff today. But tell you what has come up, Tom. Do you remember that fucker of a British journalist, guy called Fulshaw, who was getting under our skin with outrageous stuff attacking us for our climate change policies?"

"Yeah, I remember him, thought we'd dealt with the fucker though. Didn't we have something on his editor? Some scandal about a rent boy? We would keep mute as long as he kept Fulshaw mute?"

"Yeah, we did," said Bruce, "but sadly the guy confessed all to his wife and has been forgiven. So we lost our stick. That kind of coming clean is no good for us, no good at all. Anyway he told Fulshaw to take half a year out. And, from what we hear, the fool is right now cycling in Africa."

"Cycling! Cycling! In Africa! Hell, he's one of those cranks that ride a bicycle? So we're dealing here with a loser Bruce, a loser. Show me anyone who cycles, shows me anyone who walks for that matter, and I'll show you a loser. You know what, there was an old film on TV last night called 'The 39 Steps'. What a joke! They cannot be serious. No sensible person walks that far. Any more than 20 steps, I take my Hummer. Walking, cycling -- strictly for mugs, losers. So what's Fulshaw done?"

"Well, Tom, he's supposed to be taking time out, but he's continuing to write. And his most recent pieces, well, we just can't have. He says he has been talking to people who have lost their homes because of global warming that he claims the US is doing nothing about. And he makes this outrageous statement that the United States -- the greatest country on earth mark you -- is the world's most irresponsible country. Worse, he says that in the way we live we are killers, killing the poor. Lies, lies, all lies. He's made it up, obviously, lying around the pool of a 5-star hotel somewhere, with some floosie attending to his every need.

"And his stuff is not only in print, he's also on VOA -- VOA mark you, it's becoming almost as bad as that commie Bolshevik Broadcasting Corporation, the BBC. He must be in some sort of conspiracy. Cycling, forget it, just a blind."

Tom Glickmann read slowly through the piece. Reading was never his strong point.

"The fucker's gone too far, Bruce, insulting us like this, besmirching our good name. We are leading the world in tackling climate change, like we lead the world in everything else. All the money we're investing in new technologies to tackle it. He claims that we are not investing much. How dare he?"

"Tom, I guess this Fuckshaw guy is just jealous," said Bruce. "Everyone in the world wants to be an American, as you and I know, and he's mad that he's not. Everyone wants to be like us, clean living, free, healthy, good people, everyone wants to live the way we do. And look where he's from -- Britain. A pathetic country led by that pathetic Blair. I wonder if that poodle of a guy has any idea what we really think about him."

"Blair -- always bleating on about doing things through the United Nations," said Tom. "The United Nations! You and I know, Bruce, that there's no such thing as the United Nations. There's us -- one cock among 180 or so chicks that we use as and when we like. We in the US of A lead this world as we wish in the way that is in our interests. And our interests lies in conning, er persuading, everyone else that our interests are their interests too. And look at the way we spread democracy in the world, Brucie, our world, Brucie."

"Yeep Tom. Our recipe for democracy works well -- we chose someone we like to lead a government, someone who will allow our companies the right to sell their goods there without restrictions, and who will support us on the international scene. We help him -- or maybe her -- to get elected in any way we can, disapprove of him if need be, even starve the bugger of funds. And discredit anyone we don't like of course. If anyone we don't like should get elected we undermine the misguided soul in any way we can until he's thrown out and the guys we do like are chosen. OK there's one or two we're still working on -- like that fucker in Venezuela -- but we'll get them in the end. Who can match our cunning, our guile, our determination, our money....our bullets. So all around the world we have the leaders we want, saying the things we want to hear, our nice little tame puppets -- not that we let them think that of course."

"Brucie, you're a genius. With such a shrewd analysis of how we do things, you're headed for the big time my friend, the big time. You know you could go right to the top of the CIA. Yeep, we got everyone where we want them. As our unfairly maligned, great leader Richard Nixon once said -- when you've got 'em by the balls their hearts and minds will follow. No one can touch us, we are supreme."

"You know the great thing about our country," Tom went on, "is the calibre of leaders we produce, people like Dick Nixon, Spiro Agnew, Dan Quayle, the Bushs, Dick Cheney, Donald Rumsfeld. People like this give our country its greatness and its mission. Just as God shaped the world in his image, so our mission Bruce, our noble mission, is to shape the world in our image, in the image of the greatest country of all time, the United States of America."

The two men rose silently from their desks, and padded over to the large Stars and Strips flag in the corner. They put their hands on their hearts and said solemnly and in unison: "God bless America."

"You know what Brucie," said Tom, "that guy Winnie Churchill -- he was half-American let me remind you -- said in World War Two that if the British empire should last for a thousand years, this was their finest hour. Our empire Brucie, our great and noble empire, the United States, will last for a thousand years, and every day, every hour, is our finest hour."

"Quite right, Tom. And you know the great thing about our empire is that there is no danger of it becoming like the Roman Empire, no danger of us sleepwalking into decline like that did. For look what caused the fall of the Roman Empire -- people had become lazy, fat, arrogant, complacent, indifferent to the poor. They lost their morals and values. Immorality flourished. Did you know there were over 30,000 prostitutes in Rome alone? Wow, Tom, we should have lived then! Emperors like Nero wasted money on lavish parties where guests ate and drank until they became ill. Crimes of violence made the streets of the cities unsafe. The political system was corrupt, the emperor's throne was sold to the highest bidder. And it cost them more than they could afford to maintain the military to defend themselves. How different hey Tom to the U S of A today."

"Once again Bruce your analysis shows your knowledge, your wisdom, your genius. With people like you to carry the torch, our great country is in safe hands."

"Thanks Tom, you're a great judge of character, you know that? Right now I feel like getting my hands round a cream cake or two. Shall I get you one or two, or three or four or more?"

"Oh yes, what the hell, as long as I take my diet pill at the same time, it will be fine, wont it?" As the men tucked in to a box of half a dozen large cream cakes, and as Tom took an extra diet pill to compensate, they discussed what to do about that British guy called Fuckshaw, as they renamed him. Glickmann read slowly through his piece again, his already red face turning crimson.

"Our president is killing people with irresponsible policies? We are invading people's sovereignty? A peace-loving country like ours? Climate change is a greater threat than terrorism? The man's crackers, plain crackers. Off his rocker. But there's a danger that people read that stuff, hear this rubbish, and believe it. We can't let this go on Bruce, we've got to act my friend, we have got to act. Where's he heading for next?"

"Well he's been in Senegal and now he's in Mali. I think he's heading south."

"Bruce, refresh my memory old friend. Where are these godforsaken countries, Senegal and Mali? Somewhere near Brazil?"

"Not far away, Tom, but a bit further over. Over a bit of sea somewhere down there. Well a thousand miles or so over the sea actually."

"Wish I had done geography at college like you, Bruce. O.K., for starters we've got to keep close tabs on Fuckshaw. Are we monitoring his mobile?"

"Well yes, but he doesn't seem to be using it much. Keeping it for emergencies I guess."

"Well there's an emergency coming to him, we'll make sure of that. We can't have this, Bruce, can't have it. No one steps out of line like this. We've gotta fix this guy. Fix him. Scare him to death, not literally of course, we're kind people. Personal surveillance. Operation Heiki."

"Operation Heiki. I'll see to it."

The two left soon after for an early, substantial lunch in their heavily subsidised canteen. They found it best to go early, the choice of puddings was better.

And the afternoon ended, as every afternoon ended, with them taking the lift to the underground car park, climbing into their respective Hummers and driving the mile or so home. They lived in the next block to each other, so sharing a car to work would have meant too much of a walk. Just out of the question.

11

After a couple of nights in a sweaty B&B, it was time to get on the saddle again and to head east towards Mali's second-largest city, Ségou, some 90 kilometres away. After buying as much water as he could carry, David rode over the long bridge of the Niger river, with Bamako dragging on with shanty huts and vegetable gardens, spreading out miles from the city centre. Eventually the landscape became agrarian, with mile after mile of sorghum, the staple food in the area. Later, when it became more arid and drier, the sorghum gave way to millet which needs less water.

The road was flat and relatively good, running parallel at times to the river. Mostly this looked to David like a long narrow lake rather than a river. Canoes were being paddled along with poles, some of them with fishermen, others crossing the river, providing a connection between villages on opposite shores. Buses passed him, buses packed to bursting. The buses seemed to be European castoffs with sealed windows and air conditioning that probably no longer worked.

Every few miles he cycled through a village where most people smiled and spoke, although some were too bent, struggling to cope with heavy loads, to notice a cyclist. By midmorning it was hot, very hot, and by noon it was unbearably hot. He found a tree, drank gallons of water, read a book and stayed there for over two hours. He wanted to reach Ségou that evening and while the heat took its toll, and he needed to stop every few kilometres, he made it just before dusk.

David had read somewhere that Ségou is "a beautiful and relaxed riverside town... full of interesting adobe buildings and African-influenced colonial buildings... pleasant hotels and reasonable restaurants." But all he wanted was a place to camp for the night. He noticed a hostel with spacious grounds and after some discussion was told he could camp and eat there if he wished.

In colonial days Ségou was an important administrative city and a centre of agricultural development. Now it is well known to some people for its pottery, not that David was interested in buying any.

In response to low rainfall, farmers had changed to crops which grow more quickly, millet for example, he was told by the hostel warden. People had moved their livestock further south, away from low-rainfall areas, to areas where rainfall is higher. Since the late 1960s several million people had moved from Mali and Burkina Faso to Côte d'Ivoire.

"We hear there is an uneasy relation between local people and migrants," said the hostel warden. "Over-crowding is causing problems and of course could lead to serious conflict. I don't know what the answer is. It's all very unstable."

Resting later that day, David read a paper he had picked up, entitled "Survivors: the Tuareg of the Sahel"

"Over centuries," it said, "the semi-nomadic Tuareg people of Niger have adapted well to life in the Sahel's parched, marginal lands: if pastures fail in one area they move on, taking everything with them. But today increasing drought threatens the survival of even these most resilient of pastoralists. The great droughts of 1973 and 1984 decimated herds: further droughts in 1993-4 and 1997-8 thwarted recovery. Famine and poor health ensued. As food ran out, the Tuareg were forced to sell off their only assets -- their animals -- and surrender their long-term security. The Tuareg now realise they need to adapt if they are to avoid losing their traditional way of life altogether."

It was clear that as environmental migrants crossed borders in search of water security, so the crisis had become political. So-called 'water wars' were already marring relations in several regions. Climate change and the potential influxes of refugees were likely to increase tensions.

In an Internet cafe, David checked his e-mail. There was one from his editor in London, with some letters from readers attached. The editor said that he planned to print the letters and asked David to respond. The first letter read:

Dear Sir,
Your reporter David Fulshaw has got it wrong about global warming. It isn't only emissions of carbon dioxide that are causing the world to warm up -- if it is, which I doubt. No. It's also to do with sunspots. Sunspots, which have a diameter of about 37,000 kilometres, appear as dark spots within the outermost layer of the sun. Recent research indicates that the combined effects of sunspot-induced changes in solar irradiance and increases in atmospheric greenhouse gases offer

the best explanation yet for the observed rise in average global temperature over the last century. They account for up to 92 per cent of the temperature changes actually observed over the last hundred years or so.

And in any case the earth has always warmed up and cooled down. It's all cyclical. As Mr Fulshaw is a cyclist, he should learn something of cycles of temperatures!"
Yours etc.
William Rossiter Carbon,
Craggy Island

David responded:
I have to say to Mr Carbon that the notion of sunspots being a significant cause of global warming is deeply flawed. Many scientists now point out that recent studies of sunspots and global warming show no link between the two, and there are really no observations to support the idea that variations in sunspots have played more than a minor role in global warming.

Is the warming cyclical? There are some natural variations in climate, but temperatures have varied over the years within certain parameters. The temperatures we have seen in recent years are far higher than anything we have seen before. This suggests that today's changes in climate are not cyclical. But, even if they were, my articles from Africa have shown that the poor are suffering now. They are not interested in whether the warming is cyclical or not. They want to know whether we in the west will cut our emissions of carbon dioxide to lessen the impact of climate change on them. Surely we owe it to the world's poorest people to make changes in the way we live. - David Fulshaw, Mali

The second letter read:

I take the points that David Fulshaw is making, but are not carbon credits and trading mechanisms the way to deal with the climate change problem?

Yours etc

Florence Mabs,

Stokers Ferry

David responded:

Carbon credits and trading mechanisms are being pushed by transnational corporations as the answer. But they are really ways of privatising our atmosphere and climate, while doing nothing to reduce the overall level of CO_2 emissions. They allow polluters of the atmosphere to keep polluting, and are leading to massive land grabs and evictions of peasant communities so that the corporations can cultivate climate credits in the form of environmentally disastrous monoculture plantations - DF

And third letter read:

I take the points that David Fulshaw is making, and I feel pretty bad that I am contributing to the suffering of people in Africa. But my difficulty is this - what difference can I make? I am only one person. I can turn down the thermostat, leave the car in the garage, and cycle or get the bus instead, but what difference does it make? In the face of such a huge problem, I feel so helpless. Help! I need encouragement!

Helpless,

Harpenden

David responded:

I have felt like that at times myself! But no, we can make a difference. All of us. A comparison -- when we vote in a

General Election we put a cross by the name of someone. What difference does one cross make? Well, the sum of the crosses decides who represents us in Parliament and ultimately who runs the government. It's really much the same with changing the way we live to reduce our carbon footprint. One person's actions may seem insignificant, but the sum of our actions determines the future. Just as all of us in the West have contributed to the problem, so we can contribute to the solution. Don't be discouraged! – DF

The following morning David moved south, turning the pedals towards Ivory Coast, Côte d'Ivoire At dusk he came to a village which had a few shops but no bar that he could see. He pitched his tent on a patch of land close to the side of the road. Emergency supplies provided the food he needed.

Before settling down for the night, he decided to take a walk along the village street. It did not turn out to be the best of ideas. Some boys, David guessed they were young teenagers, began to follow him. He smiled, said hello, the boys laughed back and talked in the local language. David had no idea what they were saying, but had a feeling that he was being mocked. Well, ok, he thought, this is their village, I cannot complain.

Their number grew, and when David turned round to go back to his tent, the lads turned round and went with him. When he reached the tent, there were about a dozen of them. He said good night and goodbye in as many languages as he knew; the lads laughed back.

He settled down in his sleeping bag, but the lads hung around. David sensed that they were making jibes at his expense, but thought so what, they will go away eventually. The problem was, they did not go away. They came nearer the tent and David felt they were surrounding it. He began to feel nervous. Then, to a great peal of laugher, a stick was prodded on the canvass and then prodded again to more laugher. He got up, went outside and asked them to please stop doing that. Retreating a little, they laughed all the more.

David went back into his tent, but then things turned rather sinister. A stone rippled the canvas, then another and another, again to laughter and then to applause. The stones not only kept coming, they became larger, and David began to fear, not just for his tent, but for his safety. He went outside, and, this time, decided to stay there. He sat down and said nothing. The lads were thrown. There was silence. They stood there looking at him, wondering what to do. Their bravado seemed to have been broken. One of them drifted away, then another and another. Until, finally, only one was left.

The boy sat there with David for some time, before saying quietly *"Je suis desolé"* and getting up and walking away. As David went back into his tent he realised what had happened. He had been the entertainment for the evening, a Westerner who a few over-lively local lads could have a little fun with. He climbed into his sleeping bag and went to sleep.

Several more nights of camping followed, but these were spent in the grounds of bars or police stations, where David felt that he had some protection. He reached the bustling town of Sikasso in the south of Mali, and headed on to the border. The roads were often rough and the going slow. And it stayed that way after he crossed the border into Côte d'Ivoire.

Côte d'Ivoire. "Welcome to Côte d'Ivoire" read an official sign on the customs post, a post that David managed to cross without too much difficulty. Only yards further on, an unofficial sign was visible, this one in large scrawly writing: "Welcome to the land of Didier Drogba: the world's greatest footballer." It was fame, mused David, that had largely passed him by.

He now picked up a better road that led to Bouaké, the country's second largest city. Once an important slave market, Bouaké was established as a French military post in the late 1890s. Located on a plateau, the city was a market centre for a region where cotton, coffee, cacao, sisal, tobacco, rice, yams and palm products are produced.

For David, it was time for a night in a hotel. The Ran Hotel in the city centre looked like a decent place, and the bed was the best that he'd had for a while. But the room was hot, and sleep was difficult. He decided to move south the next morning, to head for the former capital and largest city, Abidjan. Checking out of the hotel the next morning, the receptionist said to him: "You're from London? Do you know our great footballer Didier Drogba, Chelsea's centre forward? Do you know that he is from Côte d'Ivoire?"

"Err, no, I didn't know that," confessed David, "although yes, I did see a sign near the border that told me. I'm afraid I don't know him. But then, London is a big place."

"But aren't you a football fan?" asked the receptionist in some bewilderment, "don't you support a club?"

"Well I'm from the north of England originally, near Manchester, and if I support anyone it's a team you may not have heard of, called Stockport County."

"Stockport County!" said the incredulous receptionist, "and you are from Manchester! Well, why don't you support Manchester United?"

Muttering something about an affinity with the underdog, David left to cycle through mile after mile of urban sprawl before reaching open country on the road south. After another sleepless night, this time in the tent, he reached the city of Yamoussoukro, Côte d'Ivoire's capital since the 1980s, but only a fraction of the size of Abidjan, the country's economic and financial capital.

Just before Yamoussoukro, David rubbed his eyes. He could not quite believe what he was seeing. At the end of a quiet side road was the bizarre sight of an enormous dome that seemed to be almost perched in the trees.

Slowly, the whole thing came into view. In the middle of the West African countryside, a large, imposing cathedral was evident, almost a replica of St. Peter's in Rome. A bewildered David had to find out more. He cycled up to the cathedral before dismounting to walk along the large and almost deserted forecourt, almost thinking he was dreaming, so bizarre did it seem.

Just five cars stood in the parking area, at least two of them belonging to food vendors. The place had a quite eerie feel.

He locked up his bike and went into the air-conditioned building; it was huge, but again there were hardly any people. He picked up a leaflet and found that he was in "Our Lady of Peace in Yamoussoukro," and that the dome measures 297 feet by 198 feet, larger than that of St. Peter's, Rome. A guide was milling around. There being no competition for his services, David requested a tour.

"Yamoussoukro is the birthplace of our country's former president, Felix Houphouet-Boigny, a great man," said the guide. "The basilica -- which is what we call it -- was his idea. He wished to express his deep love for God by means of this shrine. The land here once grew cocoa. Now it is used to glorify God."

"Workers began erecting it in 1986," he went on, "and finished the building in record time -- cathedrals can take more than 50 years to build. In September 1990, the basilica -- the largest place of Christian worship in Africa -- was consecrated for worship by Pope John Paul II. We are very proud of it."

"But how much did it cost?," enquired David.

"Well, basilicas don't come cheap, but I cannot tell you the exact figure. I don't think that has ever been revealed, although there are some estimates. And the money came from the president's own pocket. The basilica was offered to the Vatican as a gift."

Later, at an internet cafe on the road into the city, David found a feature on the Scripps Howard News Service which said that the basilica cost an estimated US$280 million -- over half as much again as the US$170 million the government spent in 1990 on health services for the country's 12.4 million people.

As he was shown round the basilica, he couldn't make up his mind whether he found it impressive or depressing. Some 10,080 square yards of stained-glass windows, some of them honouring Felix Houphouet-Boigny, were a key feature. "What if the man fell from grace," wondered David, "would those windows be replaced?"

There seemed to be more cleaners than visitors in the building. The task of polishing the marble floor must at least have been made easier, thought David, when there were so few people around. But the building seemed empty and lifeless.

A Bible was open on a stand. David looked at it and it was open at Psalm 41. He read the first verse: "Happy are those who consider the poor."

Yet did the people who built this expensive Cathedral consider the poor, he wondered? The night before, his internet research on Côte d'Ivoire had told him that the country was suffering from both political and financial instability, that illiteracy rates were as high as 95 per cent in some areas, and this, coupled with inadequate and distant health clinics, poorly maintained roads and few villages with electricity, meant that supporting a family was difficult, especially for cocoa farmers. Education was not free, so not everyone could afford to go to school, he read. And David wondered whether the money spent building the Cathedral just might have been better spent.

An elevator near the altar took him up to a gallery and outside balcony, which looked out onto a circular area bordered by colonnades, semi-circular rows of Greco-Roman columns like those at St. Peter's, Rome. A wide pedestrian way stretched beyond. But there were few pedestrians.

The guide told him that as many as 7,000 could worship there. He hoped that people would flock there from all over the continent and, indeed, the world -- "as you have done," he said.

"But how many people normally come," asked David.

"Several hundred people worship here on Sundays," said the guide, "up to a thousand on special occasions." Which still leaves six out of seven seats empty, even on special occasions David calculated as he walked back into the sunlight along the vast, virtually empty pedestrian way. One day this might be full of people, he thought, but right now he felt it was more like an airport runway with no planes. The guide caught up with him.

"Before you go, I must ask: Do you know our great footballer Didier Drogba?" David smiled, and to the guide's evident disappointment, shook his head.

"My brother, are...you....saved?," a man with a bill-board came up and asked him fiercely.

"Not sure about that," replied David, "I will need to check with higher authority." The man turned away and went up to someone else.

David bought a newspaper from a stall selling a vast range of goods. "I don't think they will have told you in there", said the vendor, pointing to the building, "that Pope John Paul agreed to consecrate the basilica on condition that a hospital was built

nearby. The Pope laid the foundation stone for the hospital --
in a field over there, you can see the stone he laid. But that's it,
the hospital has never been built."

Cycling through the centre of Yamoussoukro, and leaving it
quite late in the hot afternoon, David felt tired. Abidjan was
still 150 miles away. When he got there, David promised
himself, he would find a decent bed, take at least a few days off
the bike, take stock and decide what to do next.

A few miles south of the capital, he pitched his tent on ground
that felt as bumpy as the Himalayas. After another bad night, he
felt very tired and not in the least like cycling. Badly needing a
bed, he decided it would not be long before he looked for a
B&B.

Only a few miles further on, his back tyre punctured. "That's
it," he thought, "I'm not cycling today." Coming to a small
run-down urban area with an unpronounceable name, he spied
a ramshackle structure which boasted a sign "The Live and Let
Live Hotel". Not the kind of place or name to inspire the
enthusiasm of potential clients, but it appeared to be the only
hostelry around.

12

It was early, only a little after noon. Entering the grimy, dimly lit and deserted reception area, David noticed two things on the wall -- a tatty, unframed picture of Didier Drogba, and a tariff board which he translated as: 20€ a night for foreigners, 2000 CFA francs, about 3€, a night for nationals. Euros only accepted from foreigners. Sighing and tired, he rang a bell, an unsmiling receptionist appeared and he signed in for a room.

The rooms were down in a basement and the room doors were made of flimsy steel. When he closed the door of the windowless room, it sounded like the door of a prison cell clanging shut, rather than a door in a hotel. He lay down on a creaky, lumpy bed but was so tired he fell asleep in seconds. It was mid-afternoon when he woke. Time, he thought, to relax with a drink outside. The room was certainly no place to linger. On the way into the reception, he had noticed a small verandah in the shade at the front of the "hotel" with a couple of small tables.

To his surprise, when David stepped out there, a young woman was sitting at one of the tables, an attractive-looking woman he thought, nursing a drink. "Hi," she said in a voice that was clearly American.

"Oh, hi," he replied, "may I join you? I could kill a beer."
"Of course," she said, "I'm Lydia. Lydia Green...and you?"

"David, David Fulshaw from the UK," he said, leaning over to shake hands. "So what brings you to these parts?"

"Well, I'm a development worker with a small and little-known US agency called 'Development in our Time'. My job is to get off the beaten track and to look for places of real need, people in real need, but with the potential to escape from poverty with a little development assistance from outside. We give small grants to big-hearted people," she said laughingly, tossing her blond hair off her face, "how about you?"

"Interesting," he replied, "I must confess I've never heard of your agency. I'm an environmental journalist and I know most of the US aid agencies."

"Oh, we're very small and we don't publicise our work much. Maybe we should. You're a journalist, wow -- we should talk!" She laughed again, her gleaming all-American white teeth shining through a mouth that David could have got his bike in.

"Well, I'm supposed to be taking time off routine, but yes, let's talk," said David, happy to have someone to talk with in an eerily quiet place.

"Are you staying here," he asked.

"Well yes, just for a few nights," she replied.

"Just for the night, me. It's a bit of a godforsaken place. Look, let me get you another drink and we can talk some more."

They talked some more, and more, late into the afternoon. David explained what he was doing, about the environment refugees he had met, about how climate change was ruining their lives, change that was closely connected to the way we lived in the West. He diplomatically drew back from too much direct criticism of the US. But Lydia seemed to be ahead of him.

"The way we live and act in the States, is what you mean David. Our huge emissions of carbon and our refusal to do anything to reduce them, to sign the Kyoto Protocol, the hold the oil companies have over George W. We're a disgrace. But not all of us agree with Bush you know."

David nodded, relieved to be talking with an American who seemed not to have been taken in by their administration's policies.

"Why don't we continue this conversation over dinner," suggested Lydia, the sun having sunk below the horizon and dusk descending fast. "I've looked at the restaurant menu and can't say I hold out much hope. But I had a walk earlier, and there's nowhere else round here."

They agreed to meet later. Only a few diners were in the restaurant as the couple met, Lydia wearing a skimpy skirt and a revealing top that made David's pulse race. They looked at the faded menu whose edges were marked by grease.

"The menu apparently deserves an award for fiction', said Lydia, "People I met who stayed here last night told me that everything was off but the mutton and rice." The waitress came over. "Let me guess," said Lydia, "it's all off but the mutton and rice?" The waitress nodded, grimly. They ordered the mutton and rice, and beers.

"I've had worse beer," said David, "well, not very much worse!"

They talked about their work, their experiences, their hopes, until eventually, after some time, the meal arrived. The mutton was tough, the rice squelched around on the cracked plates. But David was hungry and was taking on fuel. Lydia ate very little.

"Well, back to our palatial suites," said David.

"Our prison cells, more like," came the response. "My door! -- is yours the same?"

"The same," said David. They went down below to their respective rooms, just a few doors away from each other. They exchanged good nights, opened and then shut their doors, awesome prison-like sounds clanging through the corridor. In David's room were two single beds with flimsy covers, a small bedside table with an old phone, but only for internal calls, and a shower/loo. He had only been in the room for a few minutes when, to his surprise, the phone rang.

"David, it's Lydia, look, I'm sorry but I feel so desperate, alone in this room, prison couldn't be worse. I can't face a night in here. I know this is rather unorthodox but...well, I have two single beds in my room so I guess you have the same in yours. Because I'm desperate for some company, I wonder if I could come to your room and have your other bed? No funny business, we're adults, we're professional people, so just for the company, purely for the company?"

"Of course, Lydia, that sounds very sensible. And after all, this is 'The Live and Let Live Hotel!'" When Lydia arrived a few seconds later, David closed the door after her, pecked her on the check and said: "Welcome to cell no 7." And while Lydia smiled, her tone was serious.

"David, you must not get the wrong idea. This hotel is so bad it's almost like being in a war zone. It pays to stay close to each other. But don't get any ideas will you?"

"If I do, Lydia, I am quite sure you will handle them," he responded smiling. "You're right, talking to each other is the way to stay sane in this place. And no embarrassment, let's use the shower room to get changed in, and, as you say, remember we're professional people."

"Fine, although I've nothing to change into. I don't wear pjs," said Lydia with disarming frankness.

"Neither do I," said David, "we can perhaps wear a towel when we come out of the shower room." They chatted, got ready for their separate beds carefully and climbed into them, just a metre apart. The light, the only light in the room was turned out and they continued to talk, and talk. Until, finally there was silence.

"I'm cold David," said Lydia.

"Africa at night can be cold," David responded, "very cold. But I didn't see any more blankets in the room. Tell you what, have mine."

"Oh no, that's not fair, you'll freeze." Silence.

"David, purely in the interests of keeping warm, you don't suppose do you that I could slide into your bed and we could snuggle up to each other too keep warm."

"Lydia, as it is such a cold night, such a very cold night, I think that would be an excellent idea." She slid naked into David's bed and pressed her body to his. Within seconds he was fully aroused.

"I take it that you have some," she asked. Indeed he assured her that he did have some as he fiddled in his bag for a 3-pack.

"We're a couple of hypocrites aren't we," he said. "I knew from the moment we met for dinner we would end up here."

"Oh I knew much earlier than that," Lydia responded, looking into his eyes, "from the moment I met you in fact. But you have to pretend don't you. You have to say plausible things. It's all part of the foreplay." The real foreplay then began in earnest, but, when movement began, the bed started to creak, to creak ominously. They heard a crack as if something had split.

"Look we can't do it here, this bed could collapse," David croaked. "tell you what....the shower. That's the best place."

The shower in cell no 7 of "The Live and Let Live Hotel" witnessed 3-pack action that night, going on with a couple of breaks until just before dawn. And while David then slumped into deep exhausted sleep, Lydia said that she wasn't tired.

13

There was no sunlight to drift into David's room and wake him because there were no windows that allowed the sun to drift through. It was the phone that jolted him out of sleep.

"It's five past ten," barked a voice that he recognised as the receptionist's, "and check-out time is ten, sharp. So we shall be charging you for another night."

"What," he barked back, "look, I could be out in five minutes."

"Too late," came the reply. "Too late. Rules is rules. More than my job's worth not to charge you."

Refraining from singing her the chorus of "Job's worth, job's worth, more than me job's worth," he enquired: "What about breakfast?"

"Breakfast ends at 9. Nobody wants breakfast after 9 o'clock," was the curt reply.

David looked at the second bed. No Lydia. No sign of her. He quickly packed his bag and went down to reception.

"Hi David," came Lydia's voice from the verandah, "how are you today?" They kissed generously.

"I'm great," he replied, "what a night, what an incredible night, you were fantastic."

"Well you were pretty good yourself my English lover," she smiled, "but I couldn't sleep, I felt too alert, so I got up without disturbing you and had a walk round. Not a bad little area, and I got talking to this guy who said that he made herbal drinks. I tasted one and it was good, very good. So I bought us a couple. They come in little individual jars. Sit down and I'll get glasses."

Lydia found glasses and poured the drinks, one from one jar, one from the other.

"Now the secret is that you knock it straight back, in one go. That way, it gives you a powerful kick," she said.

The brownish looking drinks lay on the table. Lydia picked up her glass, said cheers and downed it in one go. Cautious, ever cautious David hesitated, even looked suspicious.

"Oh come on, David," said Lydia, "down it. You can trust me can't you? After last night!"

David picked up his glass, and downed it, but not quite. In his mouth he sensed that something was wrong with it, very wrong. And while he could not avoid swallowing some of the liquid, the rest he quickly spat out, to Lydia's apparent alarm.

"You fool, why did you do that?," Her tone had changed, markedly.

"That was ghastly, absolutely ghastly," he said. But his eyes were glazing over, his head was reeling. He found himself slumping to the floor of the verandah of "The Live and Let Live Hotel". Within seconds, he was unconscious.

* * *

Feet was all he could see and hear. Feet, walking, strolling, running up and down. Slowly waking up, David's first thought was "Where am I?" He had no idea. He lay, feeling like death, on a flimsy foam mattress on a floor. But as he gradually woke up, he realised that it was not the floor of the verandah of "The Live and Let Live Hotel", a floor that he vaguely remembered hitting.

He lifted himself off the mattress, resting on his arms. "Where's Lydia?," he asked himself, and again: "Where am I?" Slowly it dawned on him that he was in a hospital. But what was he doing in a hospital?

The room, the ward, was packed full with people, some on beds, some on mattresses. "What am I doing here?" he said to no one in particular. But he was heard by a nurse not far away.

"You are here sir, in a hospital in Yamoussoukro, because you were reported to be unconscious by the receptionist at 'The Live and Let Live Hotel' just south of here. That was yesterday. You appear to have taken a drug overdose and were in a bad way. Whatever it was you took we had to use a stomach pump to get it out of you. You could even have died. What's your name? Let's get down some particulars."

"I did not take a drug overdose. I don't do drugs. I was given a drink by Lydia, a woman I met there and it knocked me out. Where is Lydia? Did she come with me?"

"Nobody came with you Mr...David...Fulshaw," said the nurse, scanning his passport, "you were found alone. Best now if you stay here for another day. Who is going to look after you?"

David wanted to say -- "I hope you are," but realised in time that patients in most hospitals in Africa arrange for family or friends to look after them, to feed them, dress them etc.

"Well if you could find Lydia for me, Lydia Green I think she said, she would look after me.... I hope," he replied. "She was staying in the hotel."

Lydia! But Lydia, realised David with a start, had given him the drink that felled him. Had she spiked it? Surely not. It must have been spiked beforehand. Lydia would not have done that. But why had she not come with him? Why had she left him?

Questions like this were racing through his mind when the nurse replied: "Yamoussoukro is a big place, we can't go looking around for a woman called Lydia Green. Think about it, and I will come back to you soon."

David lay there, wondering what on earth as going on. Where were his things, his clothes -- his bike! He was trying to puzzle it out when the nurse strode up to him.

"You are in trouble, big trouble. The police want to interview you about drug possession. They will be here any minute."

Drug possession! What in heaven's name is happening? What is she talking about? This must be a case of mistaken identity thought David.

"Mr Fulshaw? Mr David Fulshaw? We are arresting you for the possession of illegal substances and for possible drug dealing at a hotel," said the gaunt policeman who now loomed beside his mattress. "You are not obliged to say anything but anything you do say.........."

David did not hear the rest. He couldn't believe it. He was being arrested on a drugs charge, but had never taken drugs in his life. Where was Lydia? She would help him sort this out.

"Let's go," said another policeman, pulling him sharply off the mattress and clamping his wrists in handcuffs.

"But I'm innocent, I've done nothing wrong. This is all a dreadful mistake."

"You can make a full statement at the station Mr Fulshaw," half-dragging him through the ward and outside into a waiting police car, "and I would advise you to spill the beans -- as you say in England!" It was not a joke the arrested man appreciated.

The station was cramped, crowded, dingy and hot, very hot. As David, shaken by what was going on and feeling like death, was led to an interrogation cell, still handcuffed to the policeman beside him, the senior police officer repeated the customary caution and started filling in a lengthy form.

"OK, tell me your story," he said, "and start from when you arrived in Africa." And David did as he was bidden. He told everything, where he had been, what he was doing and writing and ended with his experiences at "The Live and Let Live" hotel, ending with taking a drink which must have been poisoned. The police officer listened impassionately without a word.

"Mr Fulshaw, I am less than impressed," he said when David had finished, "especially about your version of events at the hotel. I put it to you that you are lying. You told the nurse that there was a woman staying there, an American called Lydia Green. We rang the hotel and asked them to check the register. They tell us that no American woman of any description was staying there the night before last, certainly no Lydia Green."

David's eyes bulged. His mouth opened but no words came through. Gasping he eventually blurted: "but...but...that's not possible. She gave me the drink, we spent the night together...there must be a mistake, a big mistake."

"Was there a spiked drink Mr Fulshaw? Was there a woman? I put it to you that you have just told me the biggest cock and bull story -- as you say in England -- I have ever heard in my life. I suggest that you were dealing in drugs. 'The Live and Let Live Hotel' is well-known as a drug dealers rendezvous. We had it closed down for several months last year, and while we allowed it to re-open we are keeping a very close watch on it.

"I think this is what happened Mr Fulshaw. You went to the hotel to sell dugs. Your bicycle is a bit of clever camouflage. You met a drug dealer who suspected that you were offering him fakes, dangerous fakes that can kill people who take them. And indeed you were offering fakes. The dealer challenged you to take one of your own drugs. You thought you could pretend to take it but somehow get rid of it. And it went wrong. It nearly killed you. Isn't this what really happened, Mr Fulshaw?" The policeman's tone was sneering, leering.

"That's ridiculous," David was recovering and boiling, "that's pure fantasy. I have never done drugs in my life. I didn't know that hotel was a drug dealers place. God I wished I'd never stayed there. Anyway you have no proof, you could have no proof."

"We are looking for proof, sir, we are looking for anyone you dealt with. If you would like to give us a name, that might help you. Could help get you a lighter sentence." Once again the sneering, leering tone pervaded the cell.

"I have no name to give you, other than that of Lydia Green," he retorted. Lydia! Where the hell was Lydia? It was she who was the fake, it dawned on slow-on-the-uptake David. It was Lydia who had spiked his drink. He recalled the harshness of her final words to him -- "You fool, why did you do that," when he spat out some of the drink she had given him.

"Look you must find Lydia," he blurted, "it is Lydia who must have tried to poison me!"

"Mr Fulshaw, Mr Fulshaw. We are policemen, we deal in facts not fantasies. Get this into your head...there...is...no...Lydia. She exists only in your head."

There was silence, before the policeman went on -- "but I will give you one thing, without evidence we cannot charge you.

And the evidence will come, one way or the other, from an analysis of what was in your blood and what was on your clothes. If the analysis proves it was an illegal drug substance, you will be going away for a long time, a very, very long time. And most people who are in our jails for a long time, never come out, they die there."

As David's inside turned over, the policeman went on: "On the other hand, if it proves to be some kind of poison, as you claim, you may be in the clear, depending on the poison."

For the first time since waking that morning, David breathed a huge sigh of relief. The analysis would prove that he was telling the truth. But why did Lydia turn on him and try to poison him? Baffled, stunned but nonetheless glimpsing hope, David heard the policeman say: "You will kept here until the results come through. Take him away Sergeant. Who is going to look after you Mr Fulshaw?"

David shook his head and was led away, from one cell or another, to a tiny cell with five other prisoners. There were no beds, just a few thin mattresses on the floor. A tap on the wall and a bucket in the corner were the cell's only other features. "Welcome to hell," said one of the inmates; the others said nothing. They just stared ahead, alone with their thoughts. The cell was hot, the humidity even higher, and there was stench that David thought would knock him out.

He tried to make sense of what was going on, but it did not make sense, how could it make sense. He clung onto the hope that he would soon be out of there, soon be free. A woman came in with food for one of the inmates, then another and another. A warder came by. "You want food," he said offhandedly to David, "you'll have to pay for it, and pay me to get it for you. Where's your money?"

Money, bag, clothes, bike -- where was it all? He reached deep into the zipped pocket of the thin coat that he been wearing at the hotel. Relief, it was still there. At least he had not been robbed. He handed over a note. The warder departed without a word and some time later came back with food of unknown description. But David had not eaten for some time. Hunger overcame appearance and taste.

Night fell, but sleep was slow to come for the cycling prisoner, alleged drug-dealer. Mosquitoes landed on him now and again for a tasty bite. His fellow prisoners belched, snored and farted. But the thought that the analysis would prove his innocence was enough to finally help him to drift off.

*   *   *

"Heiki's screwed up," Tom Glickmann's voice was heavy as his colleague Bruce Fieldon walked into the office. "That fucker Fulshaw is still compos mentis."

"Heiki screwed up? Not like Heiki. How did it happen?" asked Bruce.

"Apparently the guy smelled a rat and didn't take all his lovely potion. So it's Plan B," said Tom.

"What's Plan B, Tom?"

"Well, the guy has already been arrested on a trumped-up drugs charge. If the charge sticks he's going away for a very long time. He won't be writing any more lies about us, not from an African jail he certainly will not. But we have to make sure it sticks. Right now an analysis of what he's taken is being done in a laboratory. It will of course show that it's our special "trouble-makers" potion, which could put him in the clear. But we have contacts in these places. A little dash -- cash to you, Brucie -- will ensure that the sample that gets back to the police is not Fulshaw's but a sample with a high level of an illegal drugs substance, a fake illegal substance. And that will see Mr Fulshaw behind bars for a long, long time."

"Tom, you are a genius, you know that?" replied Bruce; "the things that you do to uphold the integrity of the United States of America, to defeat those who would question our way of life, our values, who dare to criticise us, to spread malicious falsehoods. Take a bow Tom, take a bow. Now, to more important matters -- where are our cream cakes?"

*   *   *

Another night in the cell, a sweaty, sleepless night for the just-wanna-be-a-cyclist in Africa. Another night of bewilderment over what was going on. Another night, how much more could he take, wondered David.

"Mr Fulshaw, you're wanted in the office," said a warder who swung open the cell door and bid him come. In the office was the police officer who had questioned him.

"Take a seat Mr Fulshaw," he said, " How did you like your accommodation? We put you in our VIP suite, we like to think we are very considerate, and we thought that you would prefer a mattress to a concrete floor. I am sorry if you found it a little overcrowded. There's a bit of a crime wave around these parts at the moment and we have had to double up on prisoners per cell. But you're here -- you've survived!" David tried to force a smile but it did not come.

"Anyway," the police officer went on, "I have good news and bad news for you -- as you say in England. The bad news, and for you this is very bad news, is that the sample of blood from your body shows that you took an illegal substance, a fake substance at that."

"But that's impossible," protested the prisoner. "I didn't take a substance. I was poisoned."

"Well, the good news for you, and this baffles us, is that the traces on your clothes are different, they are indeed of a poison, say the lab people, almost similar to nerve gas. A poison that could take down your nervous system. So the samples are contradictory and we cannot understand why. Your story is that you spat out some of the drink you were given. Some went on your clothes....anywhere else it could have gone?"

"Well, some could have gone on the flower bed in front of the hotel verandah. Could I ask you to take a sample of the soil? If the soil sample has the nerve gas poison, surely that proves that I am telling the truth!"

"The jury is out -- as you say in England," the policeman was almost smiling. "OK, we will take a sample as you suggest. In the meantime, it's back to the cell for you."

Back to the cell, but back with hope. Several more grim, uncomfortable, buggy, smelly days and nights followed, his stomach performing somersaults, his arms and legs covered in bites, until a warder opened the cell door and beckoned him to the office. The same police officer was sat in a wide chair.

"The sample from the soil contained the same poison as was found on your clothes," said the officer. "We still cannot understand why your blood sample is different. That seems to confirm your story. And we have found no trace of anyone visiting 'The Live and Let Live Hotel' who was a drug dealer. We are prepared to give you the benefit of the doubt and to accept there may have been a mix-up of blood samples."

David's heart leapt, and the police officer asked his Sergeant to step outside. Alone with David, he said in a lowered voice: "Strictly off the record -- as you say in England -- that lab has been known to mix up before. The lab people will do anything for a bribe. But of course we could still accept their findings Mr Fulshaw, I am still doubtful about setting you free. I wonder what I should do. Perhaps you could help me in some way?" A bribe, he wants me to bribe him, thought David, after saying that the lab workers had been bribed. But his spirits soared. Freedom was coming.

"What would be an appropriate way to help?" he enquired. A figure was suggested that sent David reeling. "I can't afford that much," he protested, "and after all, I am innocent, I shouldn't need to pay anything."

"Oh come come now Mr Fulshaw, you are a man of the world, you know that a little grease oils the wheels." Bargaining began, but the two were poles apart. Only after being threatened with another night in the cell did an exhausted David succumb to a higher figure than he thought was

112

anything like fair. The police officer offered his hand -- "it's been a pleasure to have you in our cell, Mr Fulshaw. I do hope to see you around these parts again one day, in happier circumstances for you of course! Oh and I nearly forgot. 'The Live and Let Live Hotel' have reported to us that you left without paying your bill and that you owe them €120."

"What!" exclaimed a stunned David, bankruptcy staring him in the face; "it can't be that much."

"Well, here's the bill -- 2 nights plus food and drinks, €70, plus €50 for repairs to a bed in your room. Wow, must have been quite a night. Maybe there was a woman after all. We had better get looking for her. Anyway the hotel has asked me to collect it. I said I would be happy do that for a modest €30, which makes it €150 for you to pay. So you better pay me quick. And you should really be careful Mr Fulshaw -- not paying your hotel bill can get you into trouble with the police!"

While the police officer roared his head off at his own joke, and while David coughed up yet more money, the inevitable question was put to him. "Before you go," said the policeman, "I must ask -- I take it that you know our great footballer Didier Drogba? You don't? I am disappointed in you Mr Fulshaw, that's verging on a criminal offence! Do collect your bag on the way out,"

His bag! David was still wearing the same clothes he had worn on the hotel verandah. Enquires about his bag, his bike, had been met with a shrug. Now he was re-united with his bag. But first thing he found in the bag was his bike lock -- he had not locked up his bike. In Africa, it had hardly seemed necessary.

14

David staggered out into the light, a bright African mid-morning light. He felt dirty, the only clean part of him was that he had been cleaned out of cash. His clothes stank. He had washed them as best he could in the cell but badly needed to change them. Above all, he wanted a beer and some cement mixture for his stomach. And above else, he was free.

A roadside bar soon provided the beer. As he lingered over the best taste he had enjoyed for ages, David tried to make sense of what had happened to him. Going over everything in his mind, he couldn't make sense of it. He had met this woman, had just about the best sex of his life with her, and she had tried to poison him only hours later. Why would she want to do that? What reason could she have? Who would want to poison him, and why? And why did the hotel say she was not staying there? And that awful police cell and the trumped-up charge. What on earth was going on?

He wanted answers. And he badly wanted his bike -- where was it? He had left it round the back of "The Live and Let Live Hotel". Unlocked. He would have to go back there, he realised, and search for answers as well as for his bike. But cement mixture, a bank and a good hotel in Yamoussoukro were his more immediate priorities. He needed to recover from his ordeal.

The queue at the bank stretched for what seemed like miles and it took the released but frail prisoner a good two hours before getting any money and to feel solvent again. He decided to treat himself to a swanky modern hotel near the city centre. His room was spacious and cool, the bed was good, there was a TV and a computer in the room rather than mosquitoes. He showered, dressed in fresh clothes, drank the necessary cement mixture, and went down to the restaurant for his best meal since arriving in Africa.

An afternoon lying down watching TV seemed appealing. But he couldn't settle. His bike was out there somewhere, his companion, his mate. He had an attachment to that bike, it had been with him all the way from Dakar. It was more than a bike, it was part of him, he had to go and find it. Before leaving the room he Googled for the agency that Lydia claimed to work for, 'Development in our Time'. There was no such organisation.

In the early afternoon David once more blinked out into the sunlight. He could barely remember the name of the place where "The Live and Let Live Hotel" was situated. A few miles to the south, he told a taxi driver, who soon identified it.

"Shall I wait for you?" asked the driver, dropping him at the door of the hotel where David had nearly breathed his last.

"No thanks," he said, "I'm hoping to cycle back." And he did expect to cycle back. He trusted in the honesty of African people. No one would have taken his bike, thought David, even

115

though it was now more than a week. He walked round the back of the hotel and looked at the spot where he had left it. His bike was not there. His heart sank to somewhere around his knees. Someone had taken it. Or maybe, he fantasied, the hotel people had taken it inside for safe keeping.

He crossed the hotel's fateful verandah and rang the reception bell. A different receptionist to the one last week came through a door. "You want a bed?" he asked.

"Err, no thanks," replied David, adding under his breath that he nearly had the last bed of his life in the hotel a little over a week ago.

"I stayed here last week and left my bike at the back," he said, "have you seen it, by any chance?"

"No, I haven't seen a bike," was the blunt reply.

"Your colleague?" said David, "the woman who was on duty when I stayed. Could you ask her please?"

"No, not for a couple of days anyway. She's off." Another blunt reply.

David switched track. "I wonder please if I might have a look at your register. I would like to see if a woman called Lydia Green was staying here the night that I was."

"No, you cannot look at our register. Who do you think you are, the police? Our register's private."

David knew exactly what to do. He took out an appropriate euro note, laid it on the counter, the receptionist picked up the note and swung the register round for the non-policeman to examine. And not a word was spoken. David turned to the day he had stayed there. There was no entry for a Lydia Green.

Feeling both dejected and mystified, he nodded to the receptionist and left. He wandered around the back of the hotel again. Maybe his bike was there somewhere. After trudging dejectedly around for a few minutes, a woman suddenly tugged his sleeve, a woman he recognised as the waitress the evening that he had eaten there.

"Monsieur, monsieur," she said, "are you looking for a bicycle?"

"Am I looking for a bicycle!" he wanted to shout.

"The morning after you stayed here, I did see someone pushing a bike away," said the waitress.

"You did! Could you describe him please?"

"Well he was about 5 foot 6 inches tall, very thin, not much hair and looked as though he was a Malian. He could be a refugee from Mali. There's about a hundred refugees from Mali, living in an area not far from here, about half an hour's walk. Would you like me to tell you how to get there?"

David's heart felt stones lighter. He was getting somewhere. He took out his wallet and proffered a note to the woman to say thank you.

"Thank you, but I cannot accept that," she said, "I could not take money from a strange man. My husband would beat me if he found out."

"I know I haven't found the bike yet," David protested, "but you have been so helpful. Do you have children? Could you buy something for your children with the money?"

"I do have children," replied the waitress, "but if I bought gifts, my husband would want to know where the money had come from to pay for them. Thank you, it's kind of you, but I have to decline. Good luck with finding the bike...and there's one thing I would ask -- I can tell you're British so please could you get me Didier Drogba's autograph? That would be the best thing you could give me -- send it to me, Moira, at the hotel. My family would be thrilled!"

David smiled and assured Moira that he would do all he could. And meant it.

* * *

It was a sweaty half an hour and rather more of tottering through streets bustling with noise and people before David came to the area the woman had told him about. The stench of poverty, the dirt, the chaos, the children in torn and ragged clothes, all overwhelmed him as he walked along. Small huts and tents lay along the dusty track. There were people everywhere, a lot of people. David began to feel that he would never see that bike of his again.

A woman came up to him, and asked: "Can I help you?" A crowd of children gathered around in no time.

"Well, I'm looking for someone about 5 foot 6 inches tall, very thin, not much hair, from Mali I think, and who may have a bicycle."

The woman laughed. "Quite a few people around here are from Mali, driven from their land because the climate had changed so much they would have died if they had stayed. And there are quite a lot of people here who are 5 foot 6 inches tall, very thin, with not much hair!" The children giggled. "There are a few old bikes around," she went on, "why are you looking for one?"

David felt reluctant to say too much, thinking it insensitive to explain in that poor area that he was looking for a bike worth £1000. Anyway, he just wanted to look round himself. He thanked the woman and moved on, the children following him, some of them holding his hands and his bag. A man sitting outside his tent seemed to fit the description. But the man shook his head. "The only bikes round here are bikes that are falling to bits," he said.

On he went, everyone disclaiming knowledge of a good bike and the only bikes to be seen were very old ones. The afternoon was wearing on and David was beginning to lose hope. While sitting under a small roadside bush, with his head in his hands, a woman approached him. He explained his predicament, told her that he was looking for a refugee and an expensive bike.

"You will never see it," said the woman, "if anyone had come across a bike like that, they would keep it in their hut or tent, or it might be stolen and sold." There was silence for a while, and just as David was about to move on, the woman said slowly: "There is someone I've seen pushing a good bike, usually late in the day....come to think of it, he does rather fit the description you gave me."

David was ahead of her. A man there had his bike. Maybe the man was planning to sell it and pocket the proceeds. Even a fraction of what the bike was worth could be a large sum of money for a refugee, enough to give him a new start in life. Thoughts like this went racing through his mind.

"Where can I find him?," he asked. The woman hesitated. "I'm not sure I should tell you....If he has got your bike, would you give him something to have it back?"

"Yes, yes of course" said David eagerly, barely thinking. "Where can I find him?" Instructions were given. David was directed to a tent at the far end of a track on the left of the road.

"Hello," he said, standing outside the tent, hoping someone inside would hear. He spoke louder. There was no response. "It's a question of waiting," he thought. He was determined not to leave that spot. But after only a few minutes, a man came down the track pushing a bike -- David's bike!

"That's my bike," he blurted to the man's astonishment.

"No it isn't, it's mine. Clear off," protested the man, attempting to push it inside his tent.

"I can prove this is my bike," said David, putting a hand on the saddle, "I know the number on the bottom fork of the frame." It was a number that David had decided to memorise in case something like this happened.

Shocked, the man hesitated but continued to push the bike into his tent.

"Please, please," said David, now with both hands onto the saddle in a vice-like grip, "look at the number with me." The man began to tremble and stopped pushing.

"The number on the frame is 295921," said David, "look down at the fork and read it for yourself." The frame number was irrelevant. The man shook and said weepily: "Monsieur, forgive me, forgive me. I found this bike in town at the back of a hotel. I just thought that someone had abandoned it. As I found it, I thought I could keep it. I don't want to keep it, I can't even ride it, I just want to sell it. Monsieur, do you have any idea of what the sale of this bike could do for me here, for us here? We are refugees from Mali, environmental refugees they call us, we are desperate. Please Monsieur, don't report me, please, and please let me keep the bike."

The refugee told David his story. He said his name was Ahmed. His story was a familiar one, except that he had travelled further south, hoping to find work, but so far without success. And about a hundred people in that area were in the same predicament.

"So you planned to sell the bike," said David, "and what would you have done with the money?"

"Monsieur, I have been offered 60,000 CFA francs, and I think I may be able to get 65,000. That's a lot of money. With the money I planned to buy tools and supplies for the refugees here to use, to set up a workshop to make things we could sell in the area, things like basic furniture, chairs, tables, maybe even beds. We could make clothes, repair shoes, rear poultry and pigs, there are all sorts of things we could do. Instead of being refugees without a hope, we would be a self-employed community with a purpose."

David realised the irony of what was happening...he had seen the plight of environmental refugees, had written about them, and now one of them had stolen his bike. But stolen it to improve the life of himself and refugees like him. And had imaginative ideas of how to do it.

"So you have been offered 60,000 CFA francs for my bike," said David, working out that this was about €90. "The bike is actually worth a lot more, Ahmed. Look, I am not going to buy my own bike from you, but what I would like to do is to make a contribution towards what you have in mind -- which I think is an excellent idea. I would be really pleased to fund something like that, and would like to offer you 90,000 CFA francs."

Ahmed stared ahead, trying to take in the amount. "Thank you, thank you so much," he blurted, "with that amount of money we could do even more than I thought. I haven't much in here as you see," he said, pointing around the sparsely furnished tent, "but at least could I thank you by offering you a cup of tea?"

David accepted and Ahmed went to light some coals to boil water for the tea. It took some time and the afternoon was already far spent. By the time the tea was made, it was almost dark and David drank it as quickly as was politely possible. He wanted to ride back while there was still a semblance of light in the sky. While the bike had lights, riding after dark on pitted roads was not something that he wanted to do.

David took out the money, and also gave Ahmed his address. "Do let me know how you are getting along," he said. The men embraced, and David wheeled out his bike with a "thank you for looking after it, Ahmed. At least you did that. I might never have seen it again!"

His tyres were on the soft side, but just about good enough. He rode back along the road he had come along that fateful day at "The Live and Let Live Hotel". He was alive and had his bike....and felt great to be on it again. Dodging in and out of the traffic he arrived back at the Yamoussoukro hotel, put the bike on his shoulder and strode purposefully through the lobby to his ground floor room, to the astonishment of other guests. No way was he letting that bike out of his sight again, if he could help it. He cleaned the bike, had a beer or two and a bite to eat...and slept round the clock.

15

Abidjan, the largest city in Côte d'Ivoire, lay 150 miles from Yamoussoukro, and David was hopeful that he might talk to people there who could provide answers to what had happened to him. He would start with the British Embassy, he decided.

It was mid-March. Three days of hot cycling lay ahead, his last cycling days in West Africa, he had resolved. From Abidjan he would fly to Nairobi, stay with a friend there, and then cycle on south, all the way to Cape Town if he could. It was almost midday when he bid farewell to the luxury of the swanky hotel and turned his wheels south once again. Feeling rejuvenated, he made good progress and had covered almost 50 miles before dusk fell. Again he was given permission to pitch his tent in a police station compound. The irony of it, he thought. Once more with the police and this time very different to the last time. Police stations have their uses he thought.

The road south the next day was smooth with not too many potholes and again he made good time, pitching his tent for the night some 40 miles north of Abidjan. And mid-afternoon the next day he arrived in the metropolis, found a modest hotel, and again took his bike to the room.

The British Embassy. David felt that he needed to tell them what had happened to him and to ask Embassy staff if they could help him to make sense of it. After all, what were our embassies there for but to help British citizens in their hour of need. My taxes help to pay for these places, he reasoned.

Arriving at the Embassy the next morning, he was greeted with a longish queue, told to take a ticket and wait. And he waited...and waited. Finally, it was his turn. He was shown into a large room with a quite elderly, smart-looking man sitting at a sizable desk. While it was 35 degrees Celsius outside, the man was wearing a dark three-piece suit, a handkerchief in the top pocket, and a tie. He introduced himself as a First Officer. A younger man sat at a desk in another part of the room, his head buried in some papers.

'What can I do for you, Mr Fulshaw is it?" he asked in a somewhat harassed voice. And David began to tell this story. But the First Officer soon became restless.

"Mr Fulshaw, I am sorry about what happened to you. In this country, spiking the drinks of foreigners is not uncommon, usually for robbery and no more. But we are not a detective agency. We are here to promote Britain, especially the interests of British business, and to give people here information about Britain. We vet visa applications and so on. I cannot really throw any light on what you have told me. You should have contacted us when you were in the police station, maybe we could have helped then, when you were in trouble. But you are free now. Thank you for your interest in our work Mr Fulshaw. Now if you will excuse me, I have a lot of people to see. I bid you good day."

David was stunned. Someone had poisoned him, he had been arrested on a trumped-up charge and a First Officer of the British Embassy, his embassy, didn't want to know. Too stunned to reply, he was quickly shown the door by the younger man. To David's surprise, the man followed him out and closed the First Officer's door behind him.

"May I ask -- where are you staying?" asked the man quietly, "I could not help overhearing what you said in there and it may be worth us having a drink together later. I'm Charles, by the way. David, is it?" That at least gave David some hope. Someone cares, he thought.

The two men agreed to meet early that evening in the bar at David's hotel. David was intrigued by Charles's approach, and hopeful that he might tell him something that would help make sense of the last two weeks.

"Charles, good to see you, what are you having?" he asked as the two met that evening.

"No, I should buy you one, you're a guest in this country," was the reply. The traditional jostling over who pays went on a little, the usual pleasantries were exchanged and eventually they got down to business.

"Charles, I was intrigued by what you said earlier, that it may be worth us getting together. What did you have in mind?"

"First of all," said Charles, "What I am saying to you now is strictly off the record. You must not attribute any of this to me. Understood? OK. Well, first I feel I should apologise for the attitude of my boss. The fact is that we have become so business orientated that we have little time for anything else. And he's read your articles as I have. Rightly or wrongly, he believes that you come across as anti-American. And in view of the special relationship between Britain and US, the closeness of Blair and Bush, the collusion over the Iraq war and so on, well my boss is rather cool towards anyone who steps out of line. We just dare not upset the US of A. That's unforgivable.

"It's very little known that when Moses came down from the mountain with the Commandments all those years ago, he did not just have ten of them, no, he had another -- an 11th, this one just for Brits in the 21st century, under Blair. This one read: "Thou shalt not be anti-American. All other sins -- theft, murder, adultery, coveting your neighbour's ass, etc -- will be forgiven, but not the 11th which I give you this day."

"Makes a lot of sense, a lot of sense," replied David.

Charles picked up: "My boss was right about one thing though -- you should have contacted us from the police station. But that's history now."

"Yes, I guess I should have contacted you, but I was so pre-occupied with trying to make sense of it all that I just didn't think of it."

"OK, but tell me the full story. I only picked up parts of it," said Charles. And David related the story, said he wanted to find out who Lydia really was, a woman who had poisoned him only hours after giving him just about the best sex of his life. What was behind it all, was anyone behind this woman, who wanted to do him in?

"David, it's all related to what you're writing," came the reply. "You have upset people in Washington D.C. in high places, and, to put it bluntly, they decided to be rid of you. My last posting was in Washington, I was there for four years, and, well, you get to learn a thing or two while you're there.

"There's a secretive outfit called the Global Media Monitoring, Surveillance, Intelligence and Action Unit, GAMMSIAU. This monitors what is going on in the media worldwide that has any connection with the US. And if they don't like something, they respond. GAMMSIAU must have taken the view that what you are writing besmirches what it sees as the good name of their country. The guys there have probably been watching you for some time, but your on-the-spot articles from Africa were passionate and so critical they decided to act. They would have been monitoring your movements very closely. You were not aware of it, of course, but they knew exactly where you were at any one time, including that 'Live and Let Live' place.

"The woman Lydia was a plant," Charles went on. "She would have bribed the hotel receptionist to deny she was staying there and that would include, of course, not signing the register. It was her job to gain your trust, for you to trust her enough to take that drink as she directed. That's why she gave you great sex. It was part of her job. But your English caution saved you. You spat out some of the stuff she gave you. Then when the GAMMSIAU guys realised their plan had not worked, they switched to Plan B, to try to make out that you were a drug dealer. They would have bribed the laboratory doing the analysis of your blood to switch samples.

"But while GAMMSIAU like to think that it's very clever, it failed to realise that other samples, from your clothes, from the soil, would contradict the blood sample. And also that no drugs were found in your possession and there was no evidence of you dealing in drugs. No, those GAMMSIAU guys are not as clever as they think. They failed to cover all the bases, in baseball speak. So you were in the clear. But you were lucky mind you, very lucky.

"The poison you took would have been designed to cripple your nervous system rather than to kill you" Charles went on, "to make you non-compos mentis so that you could no longer function as a writer. It would have removed you from the scene, as far as GAMMSIAU was concerned, and there would be no dead body that people might start asking questions about."

David sat there taking it in. What Charles said made sense, he had answered the questions in David's mind. Charles could have done that in the Embassy, had he been allowed to. The Bush-Blair relationship did not allow it.

"Thanks Charles, you've answered my questions, I am really grateful to you. But I just cannot understand why the US government sees me as a threat, why they cannot take criticism, why they are so sensitive. I'm just a writer!"

"Well there's an old saying," said Charles, "a saying along the lines -- never argue with someone who buys ink by the barrel. It means don't argue with newspapers, because they can publicise an opinion like no one else can. The fact that GAMMSIAU sees critical journalists like yourself as a threat is a sign of their fear -- it is fearful that the way of life in the US is under threat. It's a sign both of fear and of weakness. On the face of it the US is the most powerful country in the world.

They are strong yes, but they are also weak because their way of life is not sustainable in the long term, it's on a weak foundation. Your articles got to them where it hurt."

"That makes a lot of sense, Charles, and nobody is going to stop me writing about what I see and experience -- this side of the grave of course! And before I leave this country, I want to write about what has happened to me, to expose these dirty tricks. I will not attribute this to you of course, but if I attribute to well-informed sources, could that be traced to you?"

"Well yes, possibly but no one could prove it," said Charles, now in a more relaxed mood. "And, in any case, I have ceased to really care all that much. I've spoken to you so openly because I happen to be leaving the service of HMG next month. I'm off to pastures new," he said with a hearty twirl of his bright pink tie.

"So where are you off to?" asked David, it dawning on him that Charles was almost certainly gay.

"Something completely different. Me and my good friend Cuthbert are going to set up as estate agents in a town in the Dordogne. A lot of British people are buying houses in the area, but there is no English-speaking estate agent in the town we have in mind. Cuthbert feels there's a gap in the market. It's going to be really nice."

Charles's tone had changed. Changed from serious and sensible into flippant and flirty.

"Well thanks Charles for all you've told me," said David, feeling just a little uneasy about the way the conversation was going, "now if you will excuse me, I'm going to get some rest and write this down."

"Oh but David, the night's still young...and you're so beautiful! You have probably cottoned on that I'm gay and while you have told me about your great sex with a woman, do I detect in you just a hint of bi-sexuality perhaps?"

Touching David's knee and moving very close to him, Charles went on: "So how about you and I getting it together and you having another great experience in Côte d'Ivoire -- and I promise I will not try to poison you!"

David pulled away sharply. "Charles, you have me wrong. I assure you that I am totally straight, 100 per cent. Couldn't be more so."

"Oh dear, what a shame. And here's me thinking that you might like to repay me for what I've told you. We could have had such a nice time. Oh well, that's life," said Charles with another wave of his tie, "I'll be off to my club then."

The men parted. David had the answers he was looking for...but felt an urgent need to leave Côte d'Ivoire without delay. First, he wanted to write down what had happened to him. He decided to draft his story the next morning when he was fresh and while the events were still jostling in his mind. Conscious that he so far had only one source for the information about GAMMSIAU, he wanted to confirm it with his old University friend, Peter Riley in Nairobi. He knew that

Peter also had some knowledge of the way US intelligence worked. His paper would insist on two sources.

Poisoned sex
from David Fulshaw, Côte d'Ivoire
"No, I am not being paranoid. But I begin this piece by telling you that the United States administration tried to cripple me, just over two weeks ago, here in the west African country of Côte d'Ivoire, Ivory Coast.

"Why, how? It seems that they do not like what I'm writing. They feel that linking climate change to their policies is to besmirch the name of their country. But I have seen it for myself. I have spoken to so many people in the last three months or so, cycling through West Africa, who have been driven from their land by changes in the climate, turned into refugees in their own country and sometimes trekking to other countries to try to survive. Poor people, people with nothing. Climate change is directly related to carbon emissions. The US is by far the biggest emitter in terms of carbon per head. And the Bush administration refuses to do anything meaningful to change that.

"Well-informed sources tell me there's a US government outfit in Washington D.C. called the Global Media Monitoring, Surveillance, Intelligence and Action Unit (GAMMSIAU). It seems they have been watching me. And decided, those charming folk, to do me in. It seems that their way of life just cannot stand criticism.

"How did they do it? By planting a woman, a woman who wanted to have sex with me so that I would trust her. I cannot say that she seduced me. No, in the crummy hotel I was staying

132

in, I wanted to have sex with her. And we did. The next morning she offered me a drink, said I could trust her after last night, but the drink was poisoned. It could have crippled my nervous system if I hadn't spat some of it out.

"Waking up in hospital I was arrested and thrown into jail......." and David went on to tell the full story. He ended it by saying: "British people, people everywhere, surely have the right to know more about outfits like GAMMSIAU. Our government should demand openness. Our Prime Minister should stop licking Mr Bush's boots -- and higher up his person -- and ask questions, probing questions. I don't for one moment suppose he will. But I do suggest that he should, and that he should come under public pressure to do so.

"One final point -- the hotel where my life as a journalist nearly came to an abrupt end was called 'The Live and Let Live Hotel'. A bizarre name for a hotel, I thought at the time. Now I realise how appropriate it is. Let's live, ourselves, yes of course. But can we live in such a way that lets others live? And that's all of us, it's about our own lives and it's about government policies. Can we let others live? Can we let live?"

David closed his lap-top and rang a travel agent. A Kenya Airways flight departing from Abidjan just after eight that evening was due into Nairobi at dawn the following day. He booked a one-way ticket from a bizarre hotel, poison, a hellish police station, a missing bike, a gay advance.....dismantled his bike and packed it in the bag. And felt thankful to be alive.

16

Letter from climate (continued). You in materially rich countries claim to be helping Africa with development aid. But I've looked at Africa and seen the ruined harvests and fields where children drowned in the floods. If through your own profligacy you wreck the climate and ruin their harvests, then you are taking away from them far more than you are giving!

Africans have a saying that they "borrowed the present from our children." But you have not borrowed the present -- you have stolen it from them and you are stealing their future. That is a crime. I am so glad that the sun and the moon are beyond reach of your hands, otherwise you could be wrecking them.

You share the DNA structure of all life on Earth. The atoms in your bodies have circulated throughout the network of living and non-living forms making up the universe. Much of what you do leaves the natural world damaged. Do you accept your responsibility for minimising this damage? Now is the time for wisdom on your part. There are many things that you can do to help slow down increases in global temperatures.

Bear with me if I go into a little detail. Your aim should be to cut down on the amount of carbon dioxide emissions that you cause; then the rate of climate change will slow down. One way you can cut down on the amount of carbon dioxide is by making fewer car journeys. Could you share a lift with a friend more often so only one car would need to be used? Driving a car is both a habit, and, I have to say, can even be something of an indulgence, bordering, in some cases, dare I point out, on arrogance. I see you, you go out of your front door, get into your car, turn the key and are delivered to precisely where you want to be. Who do you think you are? A King, responsible to no one? If a car is essential for you, then change to a smaller one or to a hybrid that uses less fuel.

Tread more lightly upon the earth, stop flying as much as you do. Ask if your journey is really necessary. Walk, cycle, use public transport. Takes longer I know. But what is time for? How about using some of it to give your children a future? Parents, if you love your children don't take them in a car to school. You are contributing to the destruction of their future.

In your home, switch off whenever and whatever you can. Warm yourself rather than the air around you. Don't leave your television or video on standby. Use low energy light bulbs, energy efficiency appliances. Switch to using renewable sources of energy such as wind or solar power. Install solar panels on your roof if it's appropriate. There are a lot of things you can do. You could also emit less carbon by using better insulation in your homes. This would lessen the need to burn fossil fuels such as coal and oil that give off carbon dioxide. Badger your government for better policies on the environment.

Your scientists are clever people. But are you clever people? Clever enough to change to stop climate change? I will speak frankly -- are you clever enough to stop your stupidity? Or will you be the age of stupid?

135

I am concerned about you, very concerned. You see, all those temperature rises may not lead to gradual change, but eventually to sudden, brutal and uncontrollable chaos. There may come a tipping point. My ice caps have so far taken thousands of years to melt, but they could go in a rush if sea levels rise too much. And high temperatures could lead to heat that sets off fires that would spread like you have never seen before. Life on Planet Earth would become impossible, you would have burned yourselves out of existence. Earth could be uninhabitable again. In the process of that happening, there would be huge suffering. And in the end you would have destroyed yourselves, your civilisation.

Will you survive? I have to tell you that 99 per cent of all the species that used to be on your planet are now extinct. There is no guarantee of your survival, not if you don't change. So I ask you -- will you be the last generation of your civilisation? I can do without you. You cannot do without me.

I would be sorry to see you go. You've been fun at times. So I plead with you -- stop climate change while you have the chance, before change descends into chaos. I have not given up on you. I remember how you humans did act on the ozone layer. Those chemicals that you were using for refrigeration and aerosols, those chloro-fluorocarbons, posed a serious risk to me because of interactions that could have destroyed the ozone layer. But when the facts became known, you acted. You insisted that alternatives be found to chloro-fluorocarbons and they were found. And in 1990 a global deal was agreed to phase them out. You acted then. Can you now act again? You have the skill and even the wisdom to save yourself. Whatever happens, I will go on, for another 13 billion years perhaps. But will you?

17

Kenya. It was one of the first countries that David had visited in Africa. It was a country he had loved from the start....but that was over 15 years ago. The capital Nairobi had since changed, and not for the better. Kenya's capital city in 2007 was widely known as Nairobbery, such was the level of armed violence and theft. David did not intend to stay there for long. On the other hand, he felt tired, very tired. When he got off the flight from Abidjan soon after dawn, he realised just how tired. It wasn't just a matter of the little rest he had on the flight, he felt emotionally drained. All the activities of the past two weeks came crowding in, bizarre activities that he had simply not recovered from, all seemed to catch up with him.

"You look shattered," were Peter's first words to David in the airport arrivals area as the two men hugged.

"I feel even worse," was the response.

"You need a rest my friend, a good rest," said Peter, on the drive to the city centre, back from the airport. "You e-mailed me some of what happened to you. Tell me the rest when you've recovered."

Peter lived in a flat in a guarded compound of Nairobi called Lavington, an area full of people who worked for non-governmental agencies. After a shower and breakfast, David slept until late afternoon. And over dinner, he told Peter the facts and showed him the draft of his story.

"I've an American colleague, Hank, who knows Washington well. I'd like him to see it. He could confirm it," said Peter. When Hank Spencer read it the next day, he smiled grimly. "Bloody awful what Bush and his cronies are getting up to. What your man in Abidjan told you is correct. I'm happy to be your second source," he said.

"David, I would advise you to be careful," Hank went on, "that outfit in Washington will still be out to get you. They will be smarting like hell that their plans have failed so far. Those guys don't like failure." Not words that David wanted to hear as he pressed the Send button to e-mail the story to his editor, and also ring Voice of America. But VOA had been warned off this British man, David Fulshaw, and would not take it.

Hank was keen to press one point on David. "Your argument is with the Bush administration which frankly will not change, and with American people more generally for the way we live. Your criticism is justified....but....you know, we can change. We can change, and some of us are changing. More and more Americans are coming to realise that we have to change, that we have to be fully paid-up members of responsible international society, that we cannot just go on emitting carbon as we are now.

"Al Gore is pointing out in a slide show that he's taking round the States that some 200 cities in the US are taking action on global warming, they're supporting the Kyoto Protocol and have become aware of the need to act. We can change, we have to change. 'Are we capable of doing great things, of rising above ourselves?' is a question that Gore is asking. We have to prove that the answer is yes."

And Hank pointed to the next presidential election in 2008, "when hopefully we will elect a president who will change our policies. There is this new kid on the block, Barack Obama, who is working hard for the Democratic party nomination. Obama was brought up in Indonesia, spent his formative years there, and his father is African. It adds up to a background of hope, the hope of much better policies."

What is climate change doing to Kenya? was a question that David was voicing.

"In many ways, climate change is affecting people in east Africa much the same as it is in west Africa," Peter told him, "more erratic weather, more floods, droughts, hurricanes and disaster situations. Many areas are now experiencing extreme droughts and famine, land is becoming less productive, water sources are drying up and livelihoods becoming more fragile. With good land being lost as far as producing food is concerned, people in rural areas are struggling to survive. And, as in west Africa, people are dying as a consequence.

"There are about 370,000 refugees in Kenya -- there could be 100,000 in Nairobi alone, many of them unregistered. Most come to Kenya from neighbouring countries, and often travel to urban areas with no documentation. They spend much of their time hiding from the authorities, struggling to make ends meet, with some women turning to sex work to earn a living.

They don't have access to reproductive health services and many refugees, especially those in urban areas who hide, do not get treatment or prevention messages.

"But the refugees, the displaced people, are not just coming from other countries. What we find is that the way of life of many of Kenya's nomadic people is under threat. Trekking from one place to another is no longer possible the way it used to be. It's reckoned that three million nomads in northern Kenya, whose way of life has sustained them for thousands of years, now face eradication. Hundreds of thousands of them have already been forced to forsake their traditional culture and settle in Kenya's north eastern province following consecutive droughts that have decimated their livestock in the last few years.

"A livestock specialist, Dr David Kimenye, recently examined how the herders are coping with drought. He talked to pastoralists in the north-east -- in five areas that are home to 1.5 million people -- and uncovered a disastrous story, a story of a huge decline in grazing land and water resources. When drought strikes, there is a lack of pasture for animals. Dr. Kimenya's study found that drought was now four times worse in some areas of the far north than it was 25 years ago. One-third of nomads living there, that's about half a million people, have already been forced to abandon their pastoral way of life because of adverse climatic conditions.

"What is worrying is that over the centuries, nomads have been able to cope with unpredictable weather patterns and regular drought, but climate change is something else. It is so severe that it's bringing many nomads to the brink of extinction.

"Today, when nomadic people move around, it often leads to conflicts over pasture land, since every other community is moving in search of pasture. Women and children, especially, also the sick and the elderly, are often left with nothing to eat. In desperate conditions, nomads have had to sell their animals and are plunged into famine.

"Cattle rustling, animals that are weak and prone to disease and emaciation, are causing big problems for the nomads. So they have been left highly vulnerable. Climate change, and the consequent recurrent droughts and lack of water and food, is giving more and more of them little option but to settle in villages. Some are completely dependent on aid handouts for most of their food. For the nomadic people, changes in the climate have ruined their tradition."

Ruin. What right did any country, any people have to ruin the traditions, the livelihoods of other people, thought David, and yet this is what is happening because of climate change.

After a few days in Nairobi, David was still feeling tired and not ready to start cycling again. Mooching was the order of the day, something that he promised himself he would do. And he read at lot. He read in particular about the impact of climate change on Africa. Peter gave him a copy of a report entitled "Climate change impacts in Kenya". This said that coral bleaching observed in the Indian Ocean and Red Sea in 1997-1998 was related to climate-change induced ocean warming on coral reefs.

"In the western Indian Ocean region, a 30% loss of corals reduced tourism in Mombasa (and Zanzibar) and resulted in financial losses of about US$12-18 million," it said. The chief coastal ecosystems in Africa -- mangroves and coral reefs -- could be affected by climate change, it went on to say. And previously malaria-free areas in Kenya's highlands could become malaria zones. Chilling, thought David. Climate change threatens people's health, makes malaria more likely.

The impact on agriculture was highlighted in another report as a life and death matter. Temperatures in Kenya were on the rise, it said, and this is causing a fall in crop harvests. Crops could not cope with very high temperatures, while more erratic rainfall was another factor. It rains a lot when it used to be dry and it's dry when it used to rain. Farmers' fields were yielding less food, and life for people had become more uncertain. It was now more likely that they simply did not know where their next meal was coming from. Chilling again.

But the reading was interrupted when Peter suggested that they visit Kibera, a Nairobi slum that had become Africa's largest shanty town and one of the largest in the world. Kibera was home to around a million people.

The original settlers in Kibera, David was told, were people from the Kenyan/Sudanese border to the north, but most people now are from the west of Kenya. They were refugees from an environment where they could not survive, unable to make a living in their homeland.

Just two mains water pipes serve Kibera, Peter told him, and residents have to pay for the water. Poverty and overcrowding mean that people are vulnerable to diseases, such as TB. In much of Kibera there are no toilet facilities, a hole in the ground being shared by up to 50 shacks. Residents of the shanty do not have access to lighting, refuse collection or government clinics or hospitals. There were none in Kibera, although some NGOs did provide health facilities. What Kibera did have was AIDS orphans, tens of thousands of them, some estimates put the figure as high as 50,000.

In the hot mid-morning sun, the two men walked down a narrow, pitted street in the shanty, music blasting from shacks crowding in on either side, children following them, some asking for money and food. A woman came out of her shack, tugged at David's shirt and said that her child was ill.

"Did you know," she said in Swahili, which Peter translated, "that there are no public health facilities here and the few private ones charge exorbitant fees. Many sick people cannot get treatment, even for simple ailments. There are a few clinics run by church organisations but they cannot cope with the demand for services. Can you help me, can you help us?"

Peter asked if they could go inside her shack; inside he gave the woman some money, and said he would raise the issue of lack of health facilities with voluntary organisations.

"There is so much need," he said to David when they were back outside on the street, "and only so much NGOs can do." A fight between a group of boys was going on at the end of the street. The kids seemed to be hitting each other with anything they could find, discarded plastic bottles, bits of wood, old shoes. It was not clear to David who was getting the better of it.

"Tempers flare very quickly in this environment," said Peter, "these kids ought to be in school -- but there are so few schools that people here can afford."

But the most significant encounter from David's point of view then followed. A man tugged his arm and said he was a former peasant farmer who had been evicted from good land in Kenya because it had been bought by a transnational corporation that planned to grow a crop that could be turned into fuel. Without a formal title to the land, the man explained that he was powerless to do anything. He was just one of many peasants who had been evicted, he said. And he had heard something he did not understand, that the the company also wanted to grow trees on some of the land to offset its carbon emissions. Could David explain what was going on, he asked?

David explained that what's happening is a scandal, that large companies were buying land in Africa to grow trees, claiming these would benefit the environment, and also to grow plants to turn into fuel. But the trees they planted were often Eucalyptus, which make big demands on water, possibly affecting local water supplies, and that the business of using land which once grew food for local people to grow plants to turn into fuel for richer people was morally offensive and just plain wrong. The companies, said David, talk about their environmental audit, but seem to have made no assessment of the impact of euclayptus trees on the local water table.

Shaking his head with apologies for what companies in Britain were doing, David left Kibera, sharing, at least to some degree, the man's feeling of powerlessness. "Every minute of the day", he thought, "every minute, when I am sitting at my laptop, riding my bike, all this is going on. Suffering, degradation, poverty that should not be happening." How insulated he was from it, he realised. How sanitised poverty was back home. He ate little that day, moved by the experience of seeing Kibera, and feeling a mixture of guilt and relief that he would walk away from it while many others had no such luxury.

Even cycling seem to lose its attractions. "How can I help those kids," he kept asking.

"For a start, don't go to pieces. Write about it, what you have seen, publicise what's going on. You are in a position to do that," said Peter. Which David did that same day. But cycling? He felt more tired than ever. He didn't feel that he had recovered from the traumas of Côte d'Ivoire.

"You know what -- you need a few days lying on the beach, total relaxation before you get on that bike again," said Peter. "Tomorrow, let's take the overnight sleeper train to Mombasa on the coast -- I know a hotel there I can book at short notice."

At 7.00 p.m. the next day, they boarded the train and enjoyed a meal and a few beers while rattling along. They slept a little, a very little, and were by the Indian Ocean the next morning. Mombasa's Bahari Beach hotel was to be home for the next few days. That at least was the plan.

18

It didn't take long for David to be on the beach, asleep. Sleeping and swimming was the pattern for the day. The following morning started much the same, and David began to feel that recovery was at last underway. By mid-afternoon he even felt a little restless and told Peter that he'd take a stroll along the beach. Peter, deep in a novel, declined to join him.

David walked along the edge of the blue water, nodding to people on the beach, enjoying the sea, the small boats bobbing about on the water, the peace, the ambience. Uplifted by the afternoon, he walked further on and the beach become much quieter, almost deserted. He revelled in the deep, unique silence of an African beach, the clear water quietly lapping the shore. An ancient Greek proverb sprang to his mind about there being no wisdom without silence.

But suddenly, within seconds, the silence was shattered by a boat with a noisy outboard engine roaring towards the shore. It stopped abruptly only yards away from David. To his astonishment, three burly men leapt out of the boat and grabbed him. Hardly before he knew what was happening, one of the men blindfolded him and put a gag in his mouth; one of them twisted his wrists behind his back and slapped them in handcuffs, the other tied his legs together. It was over in under ten seconds. And no one was around to see it.

The bound man was carried to the boat, thrown to the floor and the boat roared off. And while he could wriggle, speaking was impossible other than in gargled noises of protest. Some considerable distance from the shore, the boat drew up sharply alongside a larger vessel. The three men carried their prisoner onto the larger boat and along a passage to a small cabin. David was again thrown to the floor and the door was slammed shut. It was only minutes after he had been walking along the beach. He was a prisoner again, and once again could not even begin to make sense of it.

Lying there, he struggled, at first to no avail. His head hurt badly, he felt there were big bruises on his forehead as a result of his encounters with the floor. But the impact, he eventually realised, had done one thing, it had helped to loosen his blindfold. But how could he get it off, he wondered, without the use of hands or feet. He managed to get himself along the floor, shaking his head up and down, from right to left. Slowly, very slowly, he managed to shift it above his eyes enough to see, and then with more vigorous shaking, remove it altogether.

He lay on the floor, exhausted and bruised. He looked around the cabin and could see notices in an eastern European language, Serbo-Croatian, he thought. He knew a little Serbo-Croatian from his travels. As he lay there he could hear voices, mostly Serbo-Croatian, and one of them was a woman. And while he could not be sure, David had a feeling that the woman's voice was Lydia's.

Had those charming people from GAMMSIAU contracted to eastern Europeans another attempt to remove him, he wondered, under the guidance of Lydia?

But maybe this time they were going to kill him, he feared. They were going to dump his body far out into the ocean where it would never be found. He would be classed as a "disappeared person." He pictured his funeral. People would come to a church in London to say what a lovely fellow he was, talk about the unique contribution he had made, how he would be sorely missed....how they threw away the mold, and other loads of old cobblers.

Or maybe they were just intent on kidnapping him, he mused, take him to somewhere in eastern Europe and keep him locked up for years.

For now, however, all the prisoner felt was a quite desperate loneliness. He was on his own, totally on his own, although Peter must by now have raised the alarm, he thought. Or maybe not. He had to get out, but how?

He lay there listening to the voices and to apparent attempts to start the engine. The voices got louder and angrier and David realised what was going on -- the engine was refusing to start. That at least gave him some hope, hope that while the boat was still within sight of land and could be spotted, they would not dump him overboard. They would wait until the boat was further out for that. But he sensed that time was not on his side.

Near the ceiling of the cabin was a small window and David could see that it was now almost dark. And in the corner of the cabin was a table with metal legs, sharp-sided legs, it seemed to David. He managed to crawl over to the table and to position the handcuffs by one of the sides. It was a long shot but he began to run the handcuffs up and down, up and down. Was he getting anywhere, he wondered, there was no way he could tell; his wrists, the handcuffs, were behind his back. But it was his only hope and he kept on trying for what seemed like hours. Several times he came close to giving up. Several times he slumped exhausted to the floor. But hours later, many hours later, the handcuffs began to yield. This encouraged him to move his hands more vigorously up and down.. Until, eventually, after what seemed an eternity, his hands were free.

For several minutes he lay on the floor in the dark, shattered by his efforts. He removed the gag from his mouth and freed his legs. He looked at his watch. It was 3.00 a.m. Now what? The window. It was within his reach and he reckoned he could squeeze through it. But first of all he listened for the engine and for voices. He could hear neither, the boat was clearly not moving and his captors would be asleep, he hoped.

He opened the window slowly and quietly, and peered out. He could make out lights on the shore but guessed it was some distance away. With difficulty he managed to squeeze through the window and was out on a deck. What now? The boat that had brought him was still there, tied to the larger vessel. But the outboard had been removed. It would not have been a good idea to start it anyway, he reasoned, as it could be heard and he would be shot.

Could he get into the boat and paddle it with his arms, he wondered. No, that would hardly make the thing move very much. It was getting close to dawn and he needed to move fast; in the light he could be spotted by his kidnappers. He looked around the vessel and noticed a small life-boat. In the boat were oars. That's it, thought David. As quietly as he could, he removed the oars and climbed into the boat that had captured him. He placed the boat's rollocks in position and started to row. He was away. He was free. Or so he thought.

The shore was a long way off and he rowed vigorously. But although he was moving away from the larger vessel, he seemed to be going sideways. The shore was coming no closer. Panting for breath, thirsty, hungry, drained, he kept pounding away on the oars but was getting nowhere. He gave up rowing and sat there, feeling utterly dejected and alone.

Dawn was breaking, but David was unable to notice its beauty. What he did notice was that even without rowing, he was drifting further away from the larger vessel, while coming no closer to the shore. He was in fact going even further away. Then came a second "dawn." It dawned on him that the tide was going out. That was why he was getting no closer to the shore. And the tidal water was moving at an angle from the larger vessel, a good 60/70 degree angle, thought David. So the tide was taking him away from his captors. That was the good news, the bad news was that he could not row to the shore until the tide turned. He would have to sit there and risk being spotted by his captors.

While the tide showed no sign of turning, the captor vessel was getting further away. Maybe Peter had raised the alarm and a helicopter would be looking for him, he fantasied. It seemed unlikely in Mombasa. He sat there in a tiny boat in the Indian Ocean, being pushed further from the shore until eventually he could see it no longer. Even the vessel where he had been held was almost out of sight. David Fulshaw was alone. Would he be eaten by a shark, he wondered, or just starve to death or die of thirst. Hang on to a belief in nature, he told himself. The tide must turn.

On he drifted. But about mid-morning, he spotted something. It seemed to him to be like a pillar and the tide was taking him towards it. Getting close, he realised that it was an oil rig. His spirits soared, at last there was hope, he thought. An oil rig! The people there would surely arrange for him to be taken back to shore!

He began to row again, to speed his journey to the rig. He came within a few hundred metres of it, wondering how he would attract the attention of people on the rig. He need not have bothered. Suddenly, a searchlight dazzled him, and a voice over the tannoy blared: "Stop. Come no further. This is a prohibited area. You are under arrest."

Under arrest! Why? Before David had time to think, a small motor boat roared out from the rig, attached a rope to his boat and pulled him smartly to the rig. A security guard pointed a rifle at him, his finger on the trigger.

"Are you a spy?" a man asked curtly, after he had been taken off the boat and hauled up a ladder to the oil rig platform.

"A spy, me!" he exclaimed. "No, I happen to be journalist."

"So you are a spy then," said the man with a cockney accent, "you've come to spy on us. This rig happens to be a top government/oil industry secret. Who do you work for?"

"Look, I can explain, it's slightly complicated. But I'm so dry I can barely talk. Can I have some water please?"

Grudgingly, water was given him. And David told his story, the story of a man who had come to Africa to cycle, who had survived two attempts to nobble him, had been arrested on a false charge, and languished in a police cell for over a week.

"You know what," said the oil rig security man, when David had finished. "I don't believe a bloody word of it, not a word. They tell me there's no cod in these waters, they are too warm for cod, but you have just given me the biggest load of cods I've ever heard in my life. Those bruises on your forehead -- I wonder how you really came by those? I'm ringing the police. They will collect you...and when you get on land, mate, why don't you tell them the truth?"

The truth! What good is the truth when no one believes it, thought David. He had seen the rig and expected a refuge. Instead he was once more being treated like a criminal.

The police took their time. When their boat finally arrived, he was roughly bundled into it, feeling like a criminal, sent off with a wave from oil rig man who shouted: "no hard feelings, old boy. Drink in London sometime?"

The boat roared to the shore. Land, thought David, land, even if he was under arrest. He was again handcuffed, and frogmarched to the police station. As the station door opened who should he see inside but Peter!

"Peter!" David wanted to hug him but couldn't. "Thank God you're here. This is all so bizarre."

"What the hell happened to you?" asked Peter quietly. "I've made a statement to the police and given them some background, you tell them your story." Again David told the story, but some lengthy questioning followed. He gave the investigating policeman a description of the men who had taken him, and of the vessel he'd been kept on.

"Mr Fulshaw, you are fortunate that someone in a house overlooking the beach heard a boat engine, looked out and saw a man being grabbed and pushed into it. That was about the time you say you were taken. But it was some time before this incident was reported to us," said his investigator.. "You are free to go, Mr Fulshaw. Kidnapping in this area is not uncommon. People rowing a small boat near a top secret oil rig is uncommon, but I understand the circumstances. The gods were on your side. You were lucky. You could be dead, twice over."

"I could kill a beer -- and some food," said the freed prisoner as he blinked into the bright afternoon sun, and filled in the details for Peter as they sat in a pavement bar.

"Will those guys in Washington stop at nothing to get me?" he asked. "That boat must have been sub-contracted by them. What next?"

"What next?" said Peter, "I'm thinking that too. David, your life is in danger. Don't you think you should pack this in, at least for a while, lie low for a bit?"

"No," said David firmly, "You know the saying -- when the going gets tough, the tough get going. They are not going to put me off...but right now I need to sleep. Last night was hardly a typical night in my life."

19

Back in Nairobi, after a couple of nights recovering in Mombasa, David could not wait to get on his bike again. But Peter wasn't sure.

"David, you have been through a lot, you need more rest, and while you are in Nairobi," he said, "you must do what every other tourist does when they come here, and visit a game park." David's lack of enthusiasm filled the room. A game park did not have much appeal, and neither did he think of himself as a tourist.

"OK, you're not keen," said Peter, "but the National Park is only 20 minutes away. We'll take a cool box with some beers. Bit of luck, you might even see a lion."

They left early the next morning, taking a half-day tour. Leopards, buffalo, cheetahs, antelopes, zebras and hippos they managed to see, but not a lion. David could not help contrasting the healthy-looking animals they were seeing with the livestock of the nomads, dying of thirst. Dying, while tourists came to game parks, with barely a thought of what was happening in another part of the same country.

One more night at Peter's place was all he needed to feel ready for the off, to get the bike oiled, pump up the tyres, get his luggage together and plan the route south. It was a route following some of the Cairo to Cape Town cycle route, he hoped. A route that would take him through Tanzania, Zambia and Zimbabwe, before reaching South Africa. That at least was the plan.

Peter had a surprise for him. "Look I'm concerned about you after what's happened. I'm not sure that you should be on your own. So I've arranged with a couple of members of Kenya's Olympic cycling squad to cycle with you to the border with Tanzania -- that's about a hundred miles away and it will get you off to a good start."

Peter took him by the shoulders. "But when you are back on your own, do not talk to any strange women, be on your guard everywhere, avoid lonely places like quiet beaches, and do not trust anyone. Look at everyone as though they are out to get you. And you should also be on the look-out for drones."

"Drones?" David responded. "Do you mean honey bees or deep humming sounds? And why should I be on the look-out for either?" "David, the drones I am talking about are far more sinister. I am talking about small unmanned aerial vehicles that fly with no crew but which may have missiles. They are powered by some sort of remote engine I guess, and are controlled from a distant location. They are being used by the US military to drop bombs on enemies on the ground. OK, it's unlikely they would go that far to get you, but if you spot anything overhead that emits some sort of deep humming sound, run for cover -- quick. Although you wouldn't have much chance!"

"Well thanks for those cheering words, Peter. Sounds as if I would have more chance of escaping from a lion," said David. "Anyway, thanks for arranging those cycling escorts, sounds marvellous, and thanks for the way you've helped me here. It's been great staying with you -- give or take the little local difficulty in Mombasa."

"Just one thing about tomorrow," said Peter; "these guys from the cycling squad want to start at dawn to take advantage of the cooler weather and quieter roads. They will collect you from here."

And at dawn the following day, two supremely fit looking cyclists in their mid-twenties, lyrca-clad, lean, slim and smart, knocked at the door and introduced themselves as Amos and Jackson.

"I will never keep up with these two," thought David. But Amos was ahead of him.

"Cycling club rules apply, David, we go at the pace of the slowest rider," said Amos.

"Wonder who that will be," joked David.

"Give us your luggage," said Jackson, "we'll carry it between us." David's eyebrows shot up. These Olympic hopefuls were going to carry his luggage! Another sign of African hospitality, he thought. And perhaps mixed with a wish on their part to keep up the pace.

They wheeled their bikes to the road and began the journey south on a glorious morning. David not only had company, his mount was several pounds lighter without the luggage and he even felt that he could keep up with the fit guys, for a few miles anyway. As they rode through Nairobi's sprawling suburbs, David glanced over his shoulder at the city he was leaving. He hadn't been robbed, that was good, just kidnapped in another part of the country by people who were seemingly intent on doing him no good whatsover.

As they cycled on, the traffic became heavier and the driving was often horrendous. Amos told David about a member of their squad, a close friend, who had recently been knocked off his bike by a lorry in Nairobi and seriously injured. The lorry had not stopped, he said. The three rode through wealthy suburbs, flanked by shanty areas with beggars and street children, poverty for many, amid affluence for a few.

It was a good 20 miles before they were out into the country. The terrain was hilly, much hillier than it had been in west Africa. The countryside was dotted with shambas, small farmsteads, huts of mud on a small space of dried earth, around which vegetables, maize and fruit trees were growing. Chickens and the odd goat or two competed for space on the plots.

The land looked parched, the farm animals skinny. Further out into the country, David caught sight of wildebeest, cheetahs and giraffes running through the open fields. The trio stopped to buy water, children gathered as usual, but this time there was added excitement. Amos and Jackson were recognised. Autograph books were produced, and to David's amazement, and to much laughter at his reticence, children insisted on his autograph as well.

The road was good if bumpy, with large potholes in places. The temperature was soaring and the wind turned against them. Jackson suggested that they ride in line with him and Amos taking turns at the front. David, they said, could stay at the back of the line. It was an arrangement which suited David extremely well.

Lunch was taken at a road-side stall that was roasting maize cobs. More water was purchased, the trio took a rest, and not long after lunch, David found himself sweating heavily in the fierce heat. His clothes were dripping, his pace got slower, his legs were aching....but he was aware they were making good time, the best he had ever made, thanks to his two new friends.

It was just before four o'clock when the border with Tanzania came into sight and Amos and Jackson led David into a B+B.

"That's it, David, you have done well, almost a hundred miles. You're a good rider, you know that?" said Jackson, with Amos nodding.

"All thanks to you guys," he replied, "you've got me off to a great start."

"OK, we're staying here with you tonight, and at first light tomorrow we will head back to Nairobi," said Amos, "at a slightly faster pace than we came!"

David went in for a much needed lie-down. He had just had his longest day of cycling in Africa, and in some ways his most enjoyable. When he re-appeared, Amos and Jackson were talking to people on the street outside, signing autographs, laughing and joking.

"You need the autograph of our friend and great British rider ... David!" said Amos, to laugher and applause from the kids. Some are born great and some have greatness thrust upon them, thought David, as he signed his name in autograph books, large and small, pristine and tatty.

"Can I buy you guys a beer?" he asked his two companions. They shook their heads.

"No thanks, we don't drink alcohol," said Amos, "we're on a strict diet, both food and drink, preparing for the Beijing Olympics next year. We will have water, thanks."

Over a meal that evening, David had another surprise. "I have a couple of friends in Arusha," said Jackson, "your next big place over the border, and they are cycling up here to meet you and will ride with you into Arusha. They're club cyclists not Olympic hopefuls, so don't worry, the pace will be fine!"

David thanked them for being so considerate and got out of bed to wave them goodbye at dawn the following day. He then went back to bed. The guys from Arusha would not meet him till mid-morning, he was told, and they would collect him on the Tanzania side of the border.

*   *   *

Tanzania. Still stiff from yesterday's exertion, David wheeled out his bike after a late breakfast and pushed it along a busy street, vendors trying to sell bananas, which he bought, and cola drinks which he didn't buy. He found a shady roadside bar near the border post, had a coffee, watched the street life, and waited for the guys from Arusha to ring him.

"I'm Juma from Arusha, we're 15 minutes away from the border," a voice on his mobile eventually told him, "so I suggest you get over the border now, it will take you at least that time to get across."

The queue to cross the border was not too long and David had learned to cope with suspicious looks from border guards. He had crossed that border some ten years before, and the whole process now seemed a great deal faster than it was then.

Juma was clearly visible on the other side, together with a friend who introduced himself as Marshall. The midday sun was hot as the three made their way along the road south, the pace relaxed and the conversation easy. There is a natural fellowship among cyclists, thought David, that takes some beating.

"We're stopping with friends tonight about half way to Arusha," Juma told him, "so today's ride is only about 40 miles." Which David thought was just as well. And the following day they rode into Arusha, the city that gave its name to the renowned Arusha Declaration, a set of principles drafted by the governing party of Tanzania in 1967 as a guide toward economic and social development.

"Inherent in the Arusha Declaration", said Julius Nyerere, Tanzania's president at the time, "is a rejection of the concept of national grandeur as distinct from the well-being of its citizens, and a rejection, too, of material wealth for its own sake. It is a commitment to the belief that there are more important things in life than the amassing of riches, and that if the pursuit of wealth clashes with things like human dignity and social equality, then the latter will be given priority."

David talked to Juma and Marshall about it as they sat in Juma's house that evening, the home of all of them for the night. Juma and Marshall were not convinced that the impact of the Arusha Declaration on the country's economic and social development had lasted much beyond Nyerere's presidency, which ended in 1985.

"And the laugh of it is," said Marshall, "that Nyerere had a British adviser in the 1960s who was a member of your intellectual Fabian Society. So we think that you Brits were behind the Arusha Declaration, that it was a Fabian who helped to draft it, that Fabians were telling us how to run our country!" They laughed, the conversation moved on, and they persuaded David to take the next day off cycling to look around the city.

Arusha struck David as a pleasant, well-spaced out and quite green city. It was the headquarters of the International Criminal Tribunal for Rwanda, he was told, and this had resulted in people from many different countries moving there to assist in the trials and to enjoy a relaxed expatriate life in the bargain. He was taken to the Arusha Centre, a collectively-run organisation that provides resources on local and global social justice issues.

David heard that the Centre was committed to moving social justice forward through non-violence by providing support to individuals, member groups, and social justice movements. That it believed in an equitable, compassionate world where human dignity, the Earth and future generations are respected. That it strived to connect social, economic and ecological issues, both locally and globally.

What David wanted to find out was the impact of climate change on Tanzania. The Centre staff found him a report: 'Development and Climate Change in Tanzania: Focus on Mount Kilimanjaro'. It was a report that made grim reading.

"Analysis of recent climate trends reveals that climate change poses significant risks for Tanzania," it said; "There is a high likelihood of temperature increases as well as sea level rises." Agriculture, forests, water resources, coastal resources, human health, industry and transport could all be affected, it went on. The production of maize is projected to decline, although the output of coffee and cotton could increase.

But it was the likely impact of climate change on Mount Kilimanjaro that David wanted to know more about. The mountain was clearly visible from Arusha.

"Glaciers on Mount Kilimanjaro have been in a general state of retreat on account of natural causes for over a hundred and fifty years. Kilimanjaro has lost 86 per cent of the ice it had in 1912, and 26 per cent of the ice that was there in 2000 is gone now," read the report. "While glacial retreat globally has been linked with rising air temperatures, there is evidence that the decline of Kilimanjaro's glaciers, along with changes in the boundaries of vegetation zones on the mountain, may be due in large part to a trend of decreasing precipitation that began in the 1880s."

"It has also been found," it said, "that water from the melting of Mount Kilimanjaro's glaciers provides little, if any, water to lower elevation streams, as most ice is lost through sublimation. Water from the small amount of melting that does occur, evaporates very quickly."

"Kilimanjaro's ice cap is now projected to vanish entirely by as early as 2020," it went on. "The symbolism of this loss is indeed significant, and furthermore the loss of the ice cap would also imply that valuable records of past climates contained in its ice cores would also be irreplaceably destroyed."

The report pointed to the increased risk of forest fires on Mount Kilimanjaro "as a consequence of the increase in temperatures and a concomitant decline in precipitation over the past several decades.....A continuation of current trends in climatic changes, fire frequency, and human influence could result in the loss of most of the remaining subalpine Erica forests in a matter of years. With this, Mount Kilimanjaro will have lost its most effective water catchment," it said.

It's all tied up, thought David, when forests go, water is affected, people are affected.

"There is a critical need to develop a comprehensive and holistic development plan focusing on fire-risk and forest destruction, livelihood needs of the local population as well as on conservation strategies to ensure the long term sustainability of the valuable resources of the Kilimanjaro ecosystem," said the report.

Yes, of course, thought David, but there is also a critical need for industrialised countries to develop a comprehensive and holistic development plan that would reduce their carbon emissions, and get to the source of Mount Kilimanjaro's problems. Otherwise all the efforts of the people of Tanzania would go only a limited way to solving the problem. He talked about the report with an official at the centre. "If it continues like this, if the process goes on," she said, "then future generations will have to take our word for it that there was once snow on Kilimanjaro."

Then the official said something which surprised him. "There's another dimension to this. Farmers round here say that there is often not enough water for their crops. Most don't have irrigation, so they fill up watering cans from a tap, but it's often dry. It's not widely known that a pipeline runs from the base of Kilimanjaro to a flower-growing area in Kenya. Water from here goes to irrigate flowers sold in European countries.

"Flower plants are thirsty things, and the flowers that you enjoy in Britain may have been grown with water that should have stayed here and helped grow food for local people. I heard a British government minister, just recently, defending international trade by saying that it's environmentally better to grow flowers in Kenya than in Britain because it is warmer in Kenya. And then for Britain to buy them. But you cannot look at it in such a simple manner. It's just naive thinking. The man doesn't know the whole of it."

This was another insight that David welcomed and resolved that he must write about. It added to the sizable number of instances he had come across of international trade leaving victims in its wake. It was a trade that also played its part in climate change, responsible as it was for huge amounts of carbon emissions each day. And again there were victims.

But the official had more to add. "Changes in weather patterns seem to be causing more and more flooding in the region. This is serious for a number of reasons. It doesn't only cause crop losses, in some cases it is so severe that it changes river courses. It's happening in our neighbour, Uganda. A river, the Semliki, that makes a border between Uganda and DR Congo has massively shifted its course because of flooding. Sections of land in both countries have been lost, and Uganda has actually got smaller. That's serious, as the border is riddled with tensions as it is." We just don't realise the half of it, thought David as he left Arusha early the following day. He was accompanied by Juma for some ten miles, before he peeled off to go to work.

For the first time since Côte d'Ivoire, David found himself cycling on his own. It felt almost strange at first, but soon he picked up a good rhythm and began to enjoy his own company and cycling for cycling's sake. He remembered Peter's warning to be on his guard, and not talk to strange women. But everyone was a stranger. He had never been in the area before. He just had to judge who he could trust, who he could not trust. The people he spoke with along the way, people selling water and food, all seemed friendly and he felt safe.

He was now in the country's southern highlands, heading for Tanzania's new capital city Dodoma, which lay a good 200 miles south of Arusha. He passed numerous red-cloaked Masai tribesmen as he spun along roads with little traffic, spotting the occasional zebra and giraffe. Then it hit him. Suddenly he felt very flat. After the excitement of Côte d'Ivoire and Kenya, not always welcome he admitted, the company he had enjoyed, or at times endured, he was now on his own, and did not find it easy to adjust.

The going was slow. A southerly wind was picking up, causing him to slow almost to a halt at times. It was also erratic, almost blowing him off on a number of occasions. Crawling into a village in mid-afternoon, he felt drained and decided that was enough for the day. He enjoyed a beer and a bite to eat in a roadside bar, and pitched his tent in a police compound. Erecting it proved difficult in the strong wind.

As the just-wanna-go-to-sleep cyclist tried to settle down for the night, the wind blew all the more, and sleep proved difficult. But then at around midnight a gust of wind, such as David thought he had never experienced before, ripped the canvas from off its pegs and flung it in the air. Jumping up, he just managed to grab and hang on to a corner of the tent while the wind did its best to take it off him. After a struggle David won, but putting it up again was hardly possible, so strong was the gale. He managed to nail down a couple of corners and spent the night half in and half out of the thing.

Climate change means that winds like this are likely to get stronger, he realised, and while having your tent hurled in the air in the middle of the night was hardly pleasant, it was minor compared to the damage that fiercer winds would cause to millions of people. He was up and away at dawn, the wind seeming to have almost blown itself out.

The going was hilly and sweaty, although the rolling hills provided a wonderful backdrop, as he was now in what is known as the Masai Steppe. The roads often turned into rough tracks that were difficult and even treacherous in places. Dodoma was a further three days away, and two more nights in his tent followed. After spending them sleeping in the grounds of wayside bars, he felt thankful to eventually ride into the capital around mid-afternoon.

20

Located in the heartland of Tanzania, Dodoma became the official political capital and the seat of government in 1974 although not until 1996 did Tanzania's National Assembly move there. But the government legislature, read David, divides its time between Dodoma and the old capital Dar es Salaam on the coast.

Cycling through the city centre streets in baking afternoon heat, David found that all the B+Bs were full, probably not with Members of the Assembly but with their drivers and other staff. He rode on to another part of town and eventually found a bed for the night. He walked around, gazed at the Assembly building, but there was little else to see, other than the dust that swirled around. Few if any tourists seemed to be taking in the sights, not that there were many sights as far as he could discover.

But after a shower back at the B+B, he walked into the city centre, had a bite to eat and noticed a bar which seemed lively. As David walked in, the first thing he heard was not an African voice but the voice of an American at the far end of the bar. A very loud-mouthed American of the kind that David had heard all too many times before. And rather worse the wear for drink. Best avoided, he thought, as he settled down with a beer at the other end of the bar. A football match was being screened on a small television perched high above the bottles.

Commentary on the match was impossible to hear because of the American's loud voice. Worse, the guy was making his way over to David, having seen him enter the bar and being conspicuous as the only other white face there. To David's alarm, there was no hiding place.

"Hi there fellow," he said unsteadily, seizing David by the hand, "I'm Bill from Texas, saw you come in just now. So who are you, and what brings you to this godforsaken place?"

"Oh hi, I'm David from London," he said with lack of enthusiasm, "I happen to be just cycling through."

"Cycling, cycling!" said an indignant Bill, "you must be joking. Cycling in Africa! Forget it, forget it. Only losers cycle. Losers. Are you a loser, David? No, surely not. But, loser or not....have a drink on me. You see, I'm a winner, a winner with a big heart. Two Buds barman, and be quick about it."

"Yes, I'm an oil man, here in this godforsaken joint to try to get a concession on some of the country's oil. I don't mind telling you, David, that I could make a really fast buck in this place, a really fast buck. But you know what I'm up against my friend -- the environment ministry. The fuckers there say the plans that I have in mind for extracting oil would be damaging for the environment -- the environment, I ask you! What guy with any sense gives a damn about the environment! The environment's like cycling, David -- only losers are into it."

While Bill roared his head off, David realised that the man was talking more than he should be doing, and giving away more than he should. He decided to encourage him to talk on.

"Another Bud?" he asked him.

"I'll say," said Bill, "tell you what me old son, why don't you and I hit the town tonight and get leathered?"

"Well Bill, if I may say so, you are rather leathered already."

"Leathered already," came the response, "that's a good one, me leathered already. Ha, ha, ha." Again he rolled around, roaring loudly.

"You know what, David, I'm considered to be a very important person. You've heard of GPSs I guess, although perhaps not as you're a crummy cyclist. Let me spell it out for you. GPS is short for Global Positioning System. A lot of cars have them now. They tell you exactly where you are and how to get to where you want to go. Well, I am equipped with a personal GPS. This is linked to my company's Head Office. Tells them exactly where I am at any one moment. And if I was ever -- God forbid -- kidnapped, then Head Office would know my exact position, exactly where I was. They would alert the local police who would come and rescue me. What do you think about that, David? Aren't you impressed?"

As David did his best to nod, Bill picked up: "And talking of positions...why don't you and I sidle up to those two floosies in the corner over there. Just look at that tall one. That mouth, those tits, those legs! Wow, David, wouldn't mind getting into position on that. Not sure about her friend mind you. No, David, I don't like the look of yours!"

As another Bud-fueled roar echoed through the bar, the two women left, without Bill even noticing.

"Two more Buds. barman, two more Buds," said Bill, "so what twist are you into David? What con are you up to? All business is a twist, David, all of it a twist, so tell me your twist."

"Oh, bit of this, bit of that," David replied, feeling it better not to say too much.

"Oh you Brits, bit of this, bit of that. I reckon it's you 'bit of this, bit of that' guys who are raking in all the cash these days....I bet you're doing ok, me old son. Mind you, I bet you wish you were an American. Everyone in the world wishes they were American. The best country in the world, the best people in the world, anyone who says they don't want to be an American is just plain lying. And do you know what, I'm in the best industry in the world, the oil industry, certainly the best in the States. You know what, David, we have our government just where we want them...there."

Bill pressed his thumb firmly on the bar. "There....right under our thumb. Our government cannot do a thing unless we give the go-ahead. Not a thing. That's why the US has no time for all this environment stuff, this Kyoto protocol rubbish, this climate change nonsense. No, we'll see they stay in line. The government would never do anything to damage our interests. We tell 'em what we want and they do it. Just as your Mr Blair is George Bush's poodle, so Bush is the oil industry's poodle, Woof, woof, down boy." Another Bud-fueled roar filled the air as David probed -- "but what about the green technologies that George Bush says the US is developing?"

"Green technologies, green technologies? David, you must be joking. Public relations, me old son, solid PR. We'll see to that. Oh a few token gestures here and there but nothing to damage the oil industry. Let me tell you something -- thanks to our industry, our great oil industry, the Bush government spends less on green technologies than any other Western country. But keep that under your hat, David, under your hat."

"No, we are very comfortable in the States and we have no wish to change anything we do," Bill went on, "I run a Hummer, my wife has a Hummer, and we've just bought one for our 18-year old son. We're a 3-Hummer family, and to hell with all this reducing your carbon dioxide emissions business. Why? Because reducing our emissions means reducing our standard of living. No way, hosaay...What the fuck...where have those chicks gone? O shit."

"But don't we have to reduce our carbon dioxide emissions as a precaution   in case the scientists are right," said David egging on the oilman as diplomatically as he could, "that the world is warming and that our children will bear the consequences?"

There was a pause. For a moment the bar went quiet, Bill went quiet. He had the look of someone who could not believe what he was hearing.

"Scientists may be right?," he eventually spluttered, "the world is getting warmer? What are you, David, some sort of commie bastard? The world has always warmed up and cooled down. It's all cyclical, cyclical. More Buds barman."

"Well, it has been cyclical. But the level of carbon dioxide in the air today is far higher than it has ever been. What's happening now is not really cyclical," said David.

"By God, you are a commie bastard. Who the hell am I drinking with? And what's this about children?" Bill's mood had turned angry, very angry. "Are you telling me I don't care about my children...cycling fuckface..."

With that, he slammed his bottle on the bar and swung his right fist wildly at David's head. So wild was the swing that David had no difficulty avoiding it. But so wild was it that the oilman toppled over and tumbled to the floor on his face. And lay there...groaning.

"He did this last night," said the barman, "picked a fight. If I were you I would beat it quick before he comes round. I will see to him...and from now on, he's banned."

David left. The girl with the mouth, tits and legs was by the door and asked him if he would like a nice time. He shook his head and walked sharply to the B+B. What he had just heard he had more or less heard before from United States businessmen, similar sentiments put in a less direct way. And it confirmed his worst fears about what was happening in the US. For all its apparent strength, the George W Bush government was captive and weak, captive to corporate interests.

*   *   *

David's next destination of any size was the town of Mbala in Zambia, on the border with Tanzania. But that lay some 350 miles away, a good seven days cycling, he thought, on roads that he had been told were poor in parts, and also deserted. Wild animals could be a problem, he had been warned. A cyclist has little protection from lions and other beasts, and while David had with him a supply of pepper-spray, he was not convinced that it would offer much protection in the event of an attack by more than one animal.

He left Dodoma with a bigger supply of water than usual as he had also been warned that water supplies were tight. As his cycled out of the city, the events of last night were still very much fresh in his mind. A chance encounter, not pleasant at the time, but a useful one for his next story.

But a few miles on, he forgot all about last night. It wasn't a wild animal that nearly had him, but a dog -- a large, fierce-looking dog that leapt at him from the roadside with a terrifying growl. While the pepper-spray was still in his pannier, David's pump was handy and after waving it hopefully and as threateningly as he could at the dog's head, the intruder got the message that it wasn't welcome.

Barely minutes further down the road, he then had the misfortune to be stung by a wasp on his left arm. As the arm swelled, and cream did not seem to ease the pain, he sat at the side of road, wondering....the dog, the wasp, were they part of a biological offensive from those people in Washington D.C. who were out to get him? Surely not, he thought, but wasn't convinced.

When the pain began to ease, he mounted the bike again. While the scenery was once more spectacular, the road deteriorated, with tarmac fast disappearing. He passed through

173

the town of Iringa, the gateway to the Ruaha National Park. Along a bumpy, dusty, potholed track, the inevitable happened. He got another puncture. Getting the tyre off a wheel to mend a puncture is no cyclists favourite occupation, but David's swollen arm made it both difficult and painful.

The sting, the pain, the roads, the puncture, all contributed to the lowest number of miles that David had cycled in Africa for some time. When he rode into a village in the middle of the afternoon, he decided that's it for the day. Over a beer in a roadside hostelry he enquired if he could pitch his tent for the night around the back and this was agreed.

But as he relaxed over the beer, a policeman marched into the bar and demanded, rather abruptly, to inspect his passport. After perusing it in every minor detail, the policeman turned to the bar owner and proceeded to have a lengthy conversation with him in the local dialect. After some shaking and nodding of heads -- to David's relief, eventually more nodding than shaking -- the policeman handed the passport back, stood upright, snapped his heels together, saluted....and marched out.

"What was all that about?" David asked the bar owner.

"Oh, there have been rumours of foreigners in the area pushing drugs, that sort of thing. People from Scandinavia apparently. Not Britain. Your British nationality saved you!" Having opened up the conversation, David decided he could take it further and tell the bar owner who he was and what he was doing.

"Would you say that climate change is affecting people in this area?" he enquired.

"Yes, it certainly is," came the response, "especially the smallholders, the people with small plots of land. The weather has become hotter, the rains less certain -- in some years we barely have any. As smallholders cannot afford irrigation it means there have recently been years when they have not harvested much at all. And some people have gone hungry, very hungry."

"Has any food aid come in?" asked David.

"Yes, some food aid has come from the US and elsewhere, and obviously it's welcome in bad years," said the bar owner, "but what the smallholders would really like is aid of a different kind -- especially aid to help them develop irrigation so they are less dependent on the rain. Then they could produce their own food rather than need to be given it. They also need technology to help them store their crops after harvesting. Too much food goes to waste right now, it rots in the hot weather. And sometimes food aid has come in from the Western world and undermined our farmers. Their produce cannot compete in the market against the free food aid, and I know some who have gone bankrupt. Donors need to do more to understand the real problems of smallholders here."

David welcomed these insights and replied: "What you are saying is that aid must meet real needs, and that those needs may be different to how Western governments imagine them."

"Exactly," said the bar owner, "helping others is never easy and you have to get it right."

"Tell me, are there farmers near here who have been affected by climate change who I could speak with?" asked David.

"Well, all of them really. Let me think, there's a farmer that I know well about half a mile away, he would be happy to talk with you," said the bar owner. "The best thing would be if my son took you there. Gideon," he shouted, and a few seconds later a lad who David guessed was about 14 or 15 came through to the bar.

"Take my friend here to Musa's," directed the bar owner. The two walked down a dusty, narrow track between plots of land, David telling Gideon about the purpose of his bike ride, to arrive at a small, rather battered farmhouse. Visible was a tiny plot of maize, a plot of cassava, another of vegetables and about half a dozen skinny, squawking chickens.

Gideon introduced David, who in turn told the smallholder about his journey and its purpose.

"You are welcome. We are going through hard times," said Musa, "the rain is not what it was, we just cannot rely on it like we used to. It doesn't rain for months, and then when it comes it lashes down and even destroys rather than helps my crops. Last year the harvest only gave us enough food for nine months and we had three very hungry months. This year, thank God, has been a little better, but what does the future hold? Irrigation would help, but the cost is too high."

The two men talked on until almost dusk, David trying to understand more about Musa's farm. When David sensed it was time to leave, he thanked Musa and told him he may be drawing on what Musa had said, and asked if he could make a contribution towards the cost of installing irrigation.

"Thank you, but if we ever have irrigation for farms around here it would be on a communal basis," said Musa. "Gideon's father is trying to raise funds for a system, so please make a donation to him if you would like to."

"Well, can I donate something to you to thank you for your time and for anything you want to buy for your farm?" asked David.

"Thank you, but no, that would not be right. You're a guest on my farm, indeed you are a guest in our country," replied Musa. David felt humbled, shook hands with Musa and was about to leave when Musa went over to the chickens, picked one up and handed David the squawking bird, upside down, by its legs.

"This is for you," he said. David was thrown. Musa wanted to give him one of the six chickens he had. David's every instinct was to decline. How could he carry a chicken on his bike, he asked himself, more to the point, how could he accept a gift from someone who had so little?

Feeling overwhelmed by Musa's generosity, David stood there, desperately trying to think of a polite way of declining. Sensing the hesitation, Gideon came and whispered in his ear: "You must take it. He will be very offended if you don't." David took the chicken, now squawking like mad. He thanked Musa profusely and wandered back down the track to the bar. David felt humbled by the way a man with so little had given him something that must have been a sacrifice. While David, by contrast, was offering to give money from his relative abundance.

"What am I supposed to do with this?" he quietly asked a highly amused and laughing Gideon as he struggled with the bird.

"Don't worry, you can give it to us if you like, it can run around with our chickens." David felt deeply relieved for the offer, and, back at the bar, made a donation to the village irrigation fund.

"Tell me, where are you heading tomorrow?" asked the bar owner.

"Well, I'll be riding in the direction of the border with Zambia, Mbala. It will probably take me the best part of a week to get there, but I am in no great hurry."

"There may be no hurry for you," came the response, "but there's wildlife down the route you're planning that will be in a hurry to get you. Listen, I am deadly serious, it could literally be deadly for you. People have been attacked and not survived down that road. It's quiet and in very, very poor condition in places. And the border is 300 miles away. My friend, take my advice, I live here, do not cycle it."

"But if I don't cycle there, how do I get to the border?" asked David. There was a pause.

"Well, there's a lorry driver due here very soon now who will be driving to the border tomorrow. Buy him a beer or two, get on the right side of him, and you should be ok for a lift. Even he will be hard-pushed to make the border in a day." David did not want to give up on cycling into Zambia, it went against the whole spirit of what he was doing. But he had decided at the outset in January that the ride would not be an endurance test, or a test of survival. He did rather want to survive, and recognised sound advice when he heard it.

He met the trucker later. A burly man, about the same age as David, quiet, obviously tired. David bought him a beer at the bar, told him what he was doing, about the bar owner's advice, and asked about a lift. The trucker learned over, put out his hand and said: "Be glad of the company, but I warn you, it's an early start. Be out the front door by six sharp or I will leave without you. Only that way will we make the border in a day."

An African morning has a quality all of its own, thought David, as the truck left at dawn. Perched high on the passenger seat, his bike tucked away in the bag, the countryside, the morning light seemed to him to be utterly glorious, the atmosphere something that he could hardly put into words. "The first morning of creation, who could act rationally on such a day?" was a saying that went through his mind, although he could not recall where he had heard it. But he was also aware that as glamorous as it seemed to him, a visitor, the morning was the beginning of a hard day for many of the people that he would see and pass along the road.

The trucker stopped for breakfast at a roadside café, shook hands with almost everyone there, they bought water and bananas and continued on. The trucker, Samuel, spoke little and David frequently dozed off, but was just as frequently woken up by the truck's wheels going down a deep pothole. The journey was bumpy and uncomfortable at times, but against a background of a beautiful mountainous landscape. Finally, just before dusk, they reached the border, and crossed into Zambia, in the vicinity of Mbala.

21

Zambia. Mbala, formerly known as Abercom, is a Zambian tourist centre that could do with more tourists, said Samuel, who suddenly became talkative. It had a number of attractions, he pointed out. "Mbala has a lake -- Lake Chila -- which is only a small one, but is nonetheless good for water sports. This is also a place with a lot of history, including the slave trade, with the slave route passing through the town -- starting from Lake Nyasa in Malawi, through here to Lake Tanganyika and into Tanzania through to the coast of the Indian Ocean via Bagamoyo and finally ending in Zanzibar. More recently it has seen First and Second World War action. It's where the British fought the Germans. If you have the time, you will see evidence of fortifications and other military activities all around."

With that Samuel climbed out of his cab, waved goodbye and greeted a friend. David thanked him warmly, retrieved his bike and went off in search of a B+B. He found a rather grimy-looking one which had the advantage of being cheap. His room was small, very small, so small there was barely space to swing one of the many cockroaches that could be heard scuttling around. David picked up a leaflet:

"The Northern part of Zambia is perhaps the most interesting part of this country," he read. "This unique area is home to the great rift valley, Lake Tanganyika, the second deepest lake in the world with the highest concentration of tropical fish in the world -- perfect for scuba diving, also water sports and angling. Along the coast of Lake Tanganyika is also a National Park and Game Reserve, the Sumbu National Park with an abundance of wildlife that makes it a perfect combination for visitors."

Interesting, but I've seen enough wildlife for now, thought David, not all of it on four legs. He went out to look for somewhere to eat. But places to eat seemed scarce. He went up to a young guy who was carrying a billboard with the words "Welcome to Jesus work ministry" and asked him if there was anywhere he could recommend.

"Well, there are only two places to eat in this town," he said after a pause.

"Oh, and which one would you recommend?" asked David hopefully.

The young guy looked thoughtful and again there was a pause. "Well, let me put it to you like this -- whichever one you go to, you will wish you had gone to the other one," he said in all seriousness, "And, whichever one you go to, when you order something from the menu, don't expect to get it. A totally different dish may well appear on your table. But I would advise you not to complain."

In view of this not exactly perfect start to an evening's dining, David wondered if he should go on a fast, rather than attempt to survive either place. But he asked which was nearer, and went there. As he opened the door, he noticed a thinly-framed sign behind the bar with the rather faded words: "In God we trust. All others pay cash." Fortunately, David had cash.

To his surprise, maybe because he had not expected very much, it was not at all bad. He even got the food he ordered. And the beer was fine. But that night, his B+B was noisy. Doors were opening and closing most of the night, there was groaning and grunting, and only slowly did it dawn on David that he was staying in what was little more than a brothel.

Next morning it was back to the bike. The Zambian capital Lusaka was his next major stop. And that lay some 600 miles from Mbala, a good ten days cycling. In Lusaka, he told himself, he would take a few days off cycling. But he was beginning to weaken. As he cycled out of Mbala, the thought occurred to him that if another lorry driver offered him a lift, maybe just some of the way, he might not turn it down.

The landscape was again fantastic, but the roads and tracks were poor in parts. Heavy lorries passed him by inches and belched diesel fumes in his face. He stopped in an isolated village to buy water and bananas. An African boy of about three years old caught sight of David...and terror filled his face. He fled, panic-stricken. Do I look that bad, he wondered, or am I the first white person he has ever seen? He hoped it was the latter, but didn't think he would ever forget that look.

With the hills becoming too steep to ride at times, pushing rather than pedaling was often necessary, and the going was slow. At times he jostled with donkeys pulling carts pied high with fruit and vegetables, their owners sometimes walking by the side. At times he was alone, a deep quietness all around. At one such quiet time, in what David thought was an isolated area where no one lived, he noticed a small lake by the side of the road. It was late morning and the sun was fierce. In an impulse he stripped off his clothes and jumped into the water, taking the precaution of leaving his towel at the edge.

The water was soothing and gorgeous. He swam around, loving the rhythmic movements...when, suddenly, he heard giggling. He might have known it -- two boys had appeared from nowhere and stood there watching him. He was naked, how could he get out of the water without them seeing him naked? Hope they would just go away? No, that could be hours, he reckoned. He swam close to the edge, shouted Hi, and they continued to look at him and giggle.

He was trapped. But an idea struck him. Coming almost within reach of his towel, he pointed to an imaginary plane in the sky and said loudly -- "Look at that?" The boys looked, David grabbed his towel, covered up his essentials while climbing out of the water, and the boys continued to giggle. Picking up his clothes, he strode behind a tree to get dressed..... and the boys giggled all the more.

Well, I seem to have made their day, he thought, as he cycled off. Refreshed by the swim, he made better time, but it was hot and he soon felt sweaty again. He decided against riding too far that day. Spotting a police station compound in a roadside village, he again asked if he could pitch his tent for the night, and this was agreed. It seemed that African police quite liked to have visitors under their watchful eye.

There was a bar in the village, but it had little food. He dined on barbecued maize cobs and fruit, washed down with a beer or two. The ground where he pitched his tent was hard and David slept badly. He was on his bike again quite early the following day. He told the resident police officer the direction he was taking.

"Take care," was the response, "you will be in dense woods a lot of the time, it will be easy to get lost."

"No, I won't get lost", thought David, as he cycled off. "I've done well so far throughout this whole journey since landing in Dakar, just one or two minor wrong-turnings, but no, I won't get lost. I have a map, a compass and a good sense of direction." And he dismissed any notion of the idea that pride comes before a fall.

At first, he was riding on an open road and the sun was warm, very warm. He could see on his map where the long woods began and he finally entered them with a sense of relief. It was cool under the high canopies, and although the road had become a rough track he felt serene and happy. He recalled words of Robert Frost: 'The woods are lovely, dark, and deep, But I have promises to keep. And miles to go before I sleep, And miles to go before I sleep.'

His father had told him that the American politician Hubert Humphrey had quoted those words at the US Democratic party convention in 1960, when he was bidding for the party's nomination as its presidential candidate. Humphrey's supporters leapt to their feet and cheered for over ten minutes. Humphrey would campaign through the night, they thought. And win. But he was in bed half an hour later. And lost. Shame, his dad had told him, Humphrey seemed a decent bloke.

As for David, he was in no particular hurry. There were miles to go before he slept, and he now wanted to enjoying riding every one of them. He wanted to live intensively in the present moment. And the woods were lovely, dark and deep -- and cool. He felt he was making good progress; he stopped around noon to eat some food he had brought with him, had a nap and then mounted his bike again.

Maybe it was his nap, maybe it was because he was feeling relaxed, but about half an hour later he had a feeling that he had taken a wrong turn. He looked at his map, but could not be sure. But he felt that even if he had taken a wrong turn, he would carry on and get back on the right route. He did not want to turn back. No cyclist likes to turn back. Cyclists were prone to boast that they would rather die than turn back. But for David it did not work out as he had hoped.

The track got bumpier and became a narrow path. The bike became impossible to ride, it was too bumpy. The path then virtually disappeared. David was alone in the woods, effectively stranded with little idea of where precisely he was. It was in desperation that he eventually tried to turn back. But that did not work either. He could not find a path to take him back. And for some reason, his compass seemed to be swinging around.

He was lost, hopelessly lost. He thought back to the morning and the police officer's warning. Pride had come before the fall. He managed to steady the compass and thought the best he could do was to just head south...and eventually he would get out of the blasted woods. He struggled through the foliage, his bike over his shoulder for much of the time, his face, arms and legs getting badly scratched, his clothes torn. But he seemed to be getting nowhere, certainly not out of the wood.

Exhausted he sat down. He switched on his mobile but could not get a signal. No one knew he was there, there was no way he could tell anyone. Days later, when his body was discovered, the nice police officer would tell people: "Ah yes, I do remember a cyclist. Told him to be careful. Silly man."

Silly man. But how did he get out of it? Some words from Hansel and Gretel flashed through his mind. "I think we took a wrong turn somewhere! This doesn't look like the way... It sure is dark and scary." Dark and scary. Scared of perishing in the forest. For the second time in as many months, David's own funeral flashed before him. But this time, the "mourners," if there were any, would say that at least the wildlife had enjoyed him.

The lost soul decided that short of burning down the forest to alert people that he was there, and no doubt killing himself in the bargain, his only option was to press on. He pressed on, and on. But to no avail. The woods were just as deep, just as dark, even darker, and now it was beginning to get dark, for the afternoon was far spent. Could he survive a night, two nights, a week, a month, in these woods, he wondered? Just as utter desperation, his life's end, was staring him in the face, a tiny, very tiny path appeared in the wood. His heart leapt. David even found that he could just about push his bike along it. It must lead somewhere, he felt. And where it led was to surprise him.

The woods gave way a little, to reveal -- a single-storey house. A house! David rubbed his eyes. He couldn't believe it. Must be a mirage, he told himself. As he walked up to it and it did not disappear, he felt like going down on his knees in thankfulness. In trepidation, he knocked at the door. To his amazement it was opened by a young African woman wearing easy-fitting clothes, with jet-black hair plaited into furrows, and with quite beautiful features.

"Good heavens," she blurted on seeing this disheveled man at the door, "where did you come from?"

"I came out of the wood.... I'm lost, can you help me?"

"Lost? You look as if you've gone ten rounds with a gorilla! Look, come in and get cleaned up. You're in a bad way."

Going in the house, David had not realised that he looked so awful....until he caught sight of himself in a mirror. His clothes were torn, he was scratched everywhere, his shoes were covered in forest dirt.

"I think you'd best take a shower," said the woman, "there's a shower room along the corridor."

"Oh no, I don't want to bother you, I just want directions....to civilisation!"

"Well, we like to think we are part of civilisation," laughed the woman, "I'm Grace...and you?"

"Er, David...David Fulshaw," he said, offering his hand. "I've been cycling in Africa since January. And, for the first time in the journey, I got lost. I was so amazed to come across your house. Thank you for being here!"

"That's nice, but before we talk, why don't you take a shower and get changed -- if you have anything to change into. If not, I could lend you something."

"That's kind, but I have something in my bag, thanks."

He showered, changed and began to feel normal again. But when he came out of the shower, it was almost dark.

"I really ought to get going," he said to Grace, "could you tell me where I am?"

"I can tell you where you are, but you can't go anywhere tonight. You must stay here. We are about ten miles from the nearest village and decent road. The dirt track to the village is hardly suitable for cycling at this time of day, nor would I drive my van along so late."

"Thank you so much," was David's grateful response. "Should I pitch my tent at the back then?"

"No of course not -- we have three bedrooms here and you can have one of them. But first let me explain who and what we are, and then you can tell me how you come to be there. First of all, would you like a beer? Zambian beer is not that good, I'm afraid."

"Beer would be fantastic", replied David, and Grace explained that the house was a rural centre for a church-related development organisation that she worked for. It served as a centre that covered northeast Zambia.

"We bought this house for a song," said Grace, "almost literally. It was once owned by a colonialist who wanted a weekend retreat far away from everything and everywhere. He certainly succeeded. But he left years ago, and the house had fallen into disrepair when we took it over some two years ago. We only moved in six months back. It took a year and a half to get it into shape.

"There are three of us here. My colleagues are both away visiting farmers. I am often out too, you were lucky to find me in! We are all trained agriculturalists and it's our job to help farmers in the region to grow the food they need, and, especially in more recent times, to help them to mitigate the effects of climate change -- which are considerable."

"Wow, that fits in so well with what I am doing and what I'm finding," said David, going on to explain his bike ride, the people he had met, the effects of climate change on Africa that he had seen. He decided not to mention Lydia or kidnapping. Before he had finished, Grace said: "Look, come into the kitchen with me, you must be hungry. I was planning a meal of rice and fish plus some vegetables. You can help prepare the vegetables. Oh, your room, let me show it to you."

As they prepared food in the kitchen, and later over their meal, Grace explained more about her work.

"Changes in the climate have meant hotter temperatures and more erratic rainfall in this area, as it seems to have done in most areas of Africa. Our farmers need to adapt to that, to mitigate the effects as best they can.

"But first of all let me tell you that we were nudged into action by a report called 'Africa: Up in Smoke?' that was prepared some three or four years ago, 2003 I think it was, by over 20 development and environmental agencies in the UK including Christian Aid, Tearfund, Oxfam and Friends of the Earth. This said that efforts to alleviate poverty in Africa would fail unless urgent action was taken to stop climate change. By disrupting vital rains, bringing more droughts and floods, climate change was devastating the livelihoods of many Africans, overwhelmingly the poorest people, it said. Unable to afford irrigation, their crops depend on the rain. Livelihoods built for generations on particular patterns of farming may become unviable, it pointed out. So we decided to act.

"Our project here aims to mitigate the effects of drought through the right kind of farming and water harvesting techniques. If water is available and food output can be sustained, then people will stay in their villages during droughts. Increasing water storage for domestic and agricultural purposes is vital.

"The construction of sand dams is one of the water harvesting techniques that we recommend. Sand dams are reinforced concrete walls built across river beds, two to four metres high. They are a cost-effective, innovative solution to water shortages in semi-arid areas like this, and have the potential to really improve things for the farmer.

"In this area, the dams are helping both homes and farm plots to have water. Another rainwater harvesting part of the project is the construction of large ponds to hold more water for when it's needed, in times of drought. And rainwater is also harvested from the roofs of schools and health facilities.

"Mind you, rainwater harvesting methods like ponds are traditional mechanisms that have long helped people here to cope. But since droughts have become more frequent and severe, larger ponds are needed to store water for a longer time than before. Local knowledge has been incorporated into the project from the planning stage.

"The construction of the ponds, wells and reservoirs will mean that water is available during the dry periods and make it possible for the communities to stay in their area instead of migrating to other areas.

"Agroforestry -- you've heard of that I imagine -- is a significant part of the project. I guess you know that it is a system in which crops and livestock, trees and shrubs, are integrated, growing together in the same plot of land. It has proved to increase output, sometimes by significant amounts. Agroforestry helps both to protect and sustain land. The practice is not new, but is now seen as highly suitable for mitigating the effects of climate change.

"Part of our agroforestry work is the planting of drought resistant crops and fruit trees. To decide which crops to plant, village communities are approached for their knowledge. That's an important part of development work -- consult people from the very beginning."

"You know, this is fascinating," said David, "but you are having to do all this mitigation and adaptation work because of us! Because we in the West cannot control our carbon emissions. We caused the problem, and you -- you who did not cause it -- are having to deal with it. You are having to spend time and effort dealing with it. It is just so unjust. It's like me damaging your house and just walking off and leaving you to cope with it."

"Yes, except that churches in Britain and in other Western countries are helping us to cope, they are helping us with with funding, and are trying to persuade their governments to act on climate change. And some of the things we are doing -- like harvesting every drop of water -- we should be doing anyway. My fear, however, is that if climate change becomes worse, if, I may say, you in the West don't get your act together and cut carbon emissions, then what we are doing will not be enough to stop chaos. Climate change could, for us, become climate chaos. And a great many people would suffer."

There was silence. David was shaking his head. "This is just so unfair. I don't think that people in the UK realise that the way they live is damaging the lives of people here."

"Well, you tell them, David, you tell them. You know I don't think it was only by chance that you dropped in out of the forest today. You needed to hear what I've said and I needed to know that there are journalists like you who care and who are writing about the issues. Climate change is not high on the media agenda here in Zambia and more coverage in the international press could encourage our own media to give it more coverage. The papers need to demystify climate change, to make it meaningful to ordinary people."

"I will certainly write about this," he said. There was silence again.

"Don't forget, David, to hold on to hope," Grace went on. "The situation seems grim, in many ways, but there is hope. I was inspired on Sunday by a reading in the village church from the book of Isaiah: 'The time is coming when the Lord will make every plant and tree in the land grow large and beautiful'."

"That's lovely, but that time will be delayed because of climate change, and it's difficult to see it coming unless people act responsibly, especially us in the West," David responded.

Again, there was silence, until Grace said: "David, it's getting late and I normally end each day with half an hour's silence. I light a candle and sit in front of it, trying to empty my mind and just be at peace. You are welcome to join me, but don't feel under any obligation. Or, if you like, join me for some of the time. You look very tired and I'm not surprised after the day you've had. Half an hour may be too long, you may fall asleep!"

"You're right. I would love to join you for say around ten minutes or so and then just quietly go to bed."

They sat in silence. David felt moved by the unique calm in the room, something he didn't feel he had ever experienced. I must try silence again, he thought. But he was also exhausted and after ten minutes, got up, smiled at Grace, whispered good night and quietly left. His head hit the pillow and he was asleep in seconds.

22

David was in the habit of waking just after dawn. The light of an African morning was too bright too soon for him to sleep. This morning, he shot up in bed with a start and with an awful thought. What if Grace was another Lydia? A more cunning Lydia, out to get his trust -- only to poison him? No, surely not, he reasoned, I'm being paranoid, but as he got out of bed and dressed, he felt he could not be sure. Back in Nairobi, Peter had warned him not to talk to strange women. And here he was in the house of a strange woman. "David," he told himself, "if you are offered coffee, smell it with some care."

He could hear Grace moving around as he left his bedroom to walk down the short corridor to the kitchen. He noticed a picture frame on one of the walls. It didn't hold a picture, but a sentence which read: "My child, do not cheat the poor of their living" -- Sirach, chapter 4, verse 1.

"Interesting," thought David, "sounds as if it's from the Bible but Sirach doesn't ring a bell. Must ask Grace."

Grace swung round to face him as he walked into the kitchen. "Good morning David. How's my lovely house guest?" asked a smiling Grace, going up to David and kissing him on the cheek. "Did you sleep well?"

"Fantastic," he replied, "like a baby. That's a really comfortable bed. Best I've had for some time. I am so grateful to you."

"It's been a pleasure to have you here, David. OK, after breakfast, what I suggest is this -- that we put your bike in our pick-up van and that I drive you to civilisation, as you put it, and get you back on your route. I need to go to the village anyway to buy food and to visit a farmer over there. Right -- breakfast, we don't have that much, some passion juice, bread rolls, jam, fruit and coffee."

"Sounds fantastic," said David. But his nose lingered over the passion juice rather longer than it would normally have lingered over fruit juice. It tasted delicious, as did the rolls, the fruit and the coffee. He felt ashamed of his earlier thoughts.

"Can I ask you about the sentence on your wall, from Sirach, is that part of the Bible?" he asked over the coffee.

"Yes," said Grace, "it's from what is known as the Apocrypha. This is part of the Old Testament, but it isn't recognised by all churches and is omitted from many Bibles. In Bibles that do include it, the Apocrypha comes between the Old Testament and the New. It's part of what is called Wisdom literature and it contains many verses of wisdom."

"That verse on your wall is so appropriate," said David, "by the way we live in the West, we are cheating the poor of their living."

"As I told you last night David, write about it -- and I don't think you need much persuasion from me! And read the book of Sirach, there are many more verses like that. I have another verse on a wall in my room which reads: 'If you pursue justice, you will attain it'." David sat there in deep thought. He wanted to challenge that verse, but felt it almost impolite to do so.

"Go on, David, tell me what you're thinking," said Grace, "you are not happy with that are you?"

"Well, it's not a question of me not being happy with it," David responded, "it's great, very reassuring, it's just that it begs other questions. I may pursue justice, you may pursue justice, but we both know that powerful interests are bent on injustice. If the powerful pursue injustice, if they bribe and cheat with their money, if they abuse their power, is there not a danger that they will attain what they want, rather than we attain what we want?" It was now Grace's turn for deep thought.

"Well, first of all these words are an encouragement," she said, "they encourage all of us who struggle for justice, no matter how difficult the circumstances happen to be, they encourage us to continue on that path. But to me, and I am no theologian, this verse is addressed to us chiefly as community. If communities -- local, national, international -- pursue justice, then it will be attained. Yes, powerful interests can influence communities to move away from justice, but people who believe in justice must work to counter their power, to uphold justice, to attain it. And I have a feeling, David, that this is what your writing is about!

"But, to more immediate matters, your bike is in a dreadful state, you can hardly see it for dirt! May I suggest that after you have finished your coffee I give you a bucket of soapy water and a cloth, and a can of oil too, and that you rescue the poor thing?"

"Great idea, thank you. It needed a good lubrication anyway," he said. He blinked out into the bright morning to look at his bike, which was certainly in a poor way. But the dirt came off, the chain was liberally oiled and the bike began to resemble something like the mount he had started with in Senegal. But yesterday's scratches from the forest trees and bushes stayed firmly on, however, a lasting memento, thought David.

Back in the house he asked Grace if he could make a contribution to the organisation, "just to say thanks for your wonderful hospitality."

"Well I would rather you did that in Lusaka, at our head office. In fact you could stay there if you wish. Let me give you the address. It's the Moses Hayward Development Agency, named after our founder. It's quite near the city centre. They are involved with matters such as education and health-care, as well as agriculture."

"Thank you, I think I will do that. And Grace, can I apologise for not having a personal gift for you. I would have brought one if I'd known I was coming!"

"David, thank you for the lovely thought, but this is not an English dinner party! I tell you what you can give me in due course -- a copy of anything you write. And keep in touch. Here's my e-mail. And come again, in a planned way next time!"

"I will try to do that. I'm back at work at the start of July and will be looking at future trips. My difficulty with visits a long way from the UK comes back to the carbon emissions issue. I have flown a lot in the course of my work and I am a big culprit when it comes to emissions. My dilemma is -- how do I visit people and countries that I need to visit, without flying -- especially if they are in southern Africa!"

"Well, don't be too hard on yourself David, you need to fly to do your work, to tell people something of how life is here in Africa, to publicise what is going on. In your type of work, you can maybe do more good by flying than not flying!" Giving David a hug of reassurance, Grace added, "come on, let's get going."

They hauled the bike onto the pick-up van and set off along the dusty, bumpy, pot-holed track. David was thrown around so much he felt at times as if his bones would not survive.

"You know. I reckon you were not far off this track yesterday," said Grace. "If you had turned west, rather than kept going due south, you would have found it. But then we would never have met!"

The ten miles to the village took almost 40 minutes so poor was the track. But eventually a traditional African village came into view, the fruit sellers, stalls with various wares, bars, they were all there, and above all, thought David, a road!

"Well here we are David," said Grace, "God speed the rest of your journey. And take care now, These roads can be dangerous. And don't get lost!"

Another hug followed. "You know, I really do hope to see you again, David, and I mean it."

"And I want to see you again, Grace, in more normal circumstances. And I mean it."

As Grace drove away, David felt lost. He got on well with most people but had felt an affinity with Grace that was different. He had been half-hoping that she would suggest that he stayed on for a few more days, He almost felt as if he had fallen in love. "Stupid," he told himself, "I doubt if I will ever see her again."

There was a bar close by and David decided he needed a coffee and a close look at the map before setting off. He was now heading for Ndola, a city in the heart of Zambia's copper-mining region. Ndola was a good 200 miles away but the road looked good, and David thought that maybe three days, four at the most, would do it. He bought water and fruit and cycled off, the fierce hot sun beating down on the rider. As usual, the going was slower than hoped for.

The road was narrow, but the surface was good, although the lorry traffic heavy. At times he struggled to breathe as huge lorries belched past, emitting a level of fumes that David felt must be illegal. He stopped frequently to drink water. The road became hillier and more winding, the cycling was harder and at times frightening. Heavy lorries were sometimes passing him at speed with only inches to spare.

As he rounded a bend up a slight incline, to his horror a heavy lorry was coming towards him fast on his side of the road. Overtaking another vehicle, it showed no signs of slowing down. Instinctively he leapt for the grass verge but the lorry was upon him. He just about managed to get himself and most of his bike onto the verge, but not his front wheel. The huge nearside front wheel of the lorry went over the bike's front wheel -- and virtually crushed it. There was a bang as the tyre blew up. The lorry did not stop.

David lay there, stunned. He looked at his wheel. It was in a desperate state, twisted almost beyond repair. "O God what am I to do now?" he thought. A lorry on his side of the road pulled over and stopped beside him.

"Are you alright?" asked the driver, "I saw what happened. That maniac. You're lucky to be alive!"

"I'm alright," replied David, "shocked, but ok. But look at my front wheel. Wrecked. There's no way I can repair it and ride the bike."

"Well, you'd better put your bike on my lorry. I'm going as far as Ndola -- that any good to you?" asked the driver.

"That would be fantastic, thank you," said a relieved David.

"I've seen many an accident on this road," said the lorry driver as they moved off, "you're a brave man to cycle along it. Not something I would do."

"I won't be doing it again either," said David: "Tell me, do you know if there are any bike shops in Ndola where I could buy a new wheel?" The driver was doubtful, said that David might have to go to Lusaka for that, or maybe wait in Ndola while one was ordered.

As they journeyed on, the green countryside eventually gave way to mining country, mile after mile of copper mines. Copper was Zambia's chief export and Ndola was the centre of it all. It was late afternoon when they arrived in the city, the driver dropping David off by a bike shop. The front wheel of the bike was so damaged that it had jammed in the forks and it was with some difficulty that David lifted it into the shop, the forks bent and badly scratched.

After a struggle, a mechanic freed the wheel but said it was totally beyond repair. A new one? Not that size, he said, they could get one but it might take some time. Lusaka was David's best bet, he thought. It was too late in the day now, but in the morning a European-style express bus would leave for Lusaka. He should reserve a seat today, he was told.

David found the bus office, reserved a seat and sought out a B +B for the night. He found a small place, and was told that he had got the last room. The room was quite large with an interesting layout, a long way from standard hotel layout, but rather with a bed in one corner and another behind a screen, some distance away.

And the B+B had the advantage of being near the bus station. He decided to put his bike in the bag and to throw away the front wheel, with some regret, but he faced up to the fact that it was now useless.

After a beer and a bite to eat, he planned an early night. But he was no sooner in the room when the hotel's internal phone rang.

"Excuse me sir, but we have a problem," said a voice which David recognised as the receptionist's. "We are in the embarrassing position of having double-booked your room. A man has just arrived, an American, who booked a room with us some months ago. Owing to a mix-up, we let his room to you. We have checked everywhere but there are just no other beds in town tonight. We don't like asking you this, but as you have two beds in your room, we wonder please if you would let him have the bed behind the screen? Obviously, the room rate to you would be halved."

At David's end there was silence. He could not believe it. He was being asked to share his room with an American, while the experience in Dodoma was still fresh in his mind, and while the last American he had shared a room with had poisoned him. Every instinct within him cried out to decline.

"Well I just don't think I can really," he said as diplomatically as he could, "I'm very tired and need an early night." This time, there was silence at the receptionist's end. Then it occurred to David that last night he had been the recipient of hospitality. He was in need, and a stranger had taken him in for the night. Now he was now being asked to do the same. He wavered, before saying: "I will come down to reception and meet him."

He walked slowly down the stairs in some turmoil. This might be another CIA plot. The man might strangle him in his bed, be up to all sorts of things. How could he trust him, he mused. But at least he would be behind a screen, and did not the unwritten rules of hospitality demand that he share?

There was only one man in the small reception area. To David's relief, the man who wished to share his room appeared to be a backpacker, rather than a businessman.

"Hello, I am sorry to disturb you and it's kind of you to come down to meet me," said the man quietly; "My name is Edgar and I'm all ready to crash out for the night. If I could share your room, I promise that I will not disturb you."

Something in the man's words reassured David who felt that he could not say no. But on a bed a deal less comfortable than last night, and with a stranger in his room, even if he was behind a screen, David did not sleep well.

At dawn, to his surprise, the silence of the morning was broken by an unexpected sound -- voices chanting a song in the street and drums beating a tune. He looked out of his window and could see a group of people marching, singing and banging on drums as they strolled along. David guessed that they were singing in a local language, but whatever it was, it added up to a lovely sound to start the day.

He and Edgar had shared only a few words last night, but went down for breakfast together. Over the coffee and toast, they talked about their jobs. Edgar explained that he was taking a vacation from his job of promoting the use of green technologies in the United States.

"If only the Bush administration had the vision to see the opportunities, the business opportunities in green technologies, they would totally change their policies on climate change. The US is disliked, even hated round the world, for its policies, its refusal to cut carbon emissions. And yet in our economy, a huge economy as you know, there are massive opportunities."

He went on to talk of green building technologies. "Green building is one of the most important environmental issues of our time. Buildings produce 40 per cent of our carbon emissions, 40 per cent of our solid waste, and consume 40 per cent of our energy. There are now literally hundreds of new technologies and innovations in clean and green technology. If these are picked up, the US could substantially reduce its emissions and create many thousands of jobs. Climate change demands that we act. And buildings are just one issue."

Edgar spoke of vehicles and the opportunities for green technology. "Today's engines can be readily converted to run on a variety of fuels, including hydrogen. Hydrogen fuel cells used to power cars with electric motors are two to three times more efficient than petrol-fueled internal combustion engines. Moreover, they have zero-emissions and, because they have few moving parts, are quiet and vibration-free. Hydrogen is one of the most plentiful elements in the universe. It can be extracted from natural gas, coal, crude oil, etc., but water is the only pollution-free source of hydrogen.

"The hydrogen and oxygen atoms in water can be easily and cleanly split apart by electrolysis, ideally using electricity from clean sources, such as solar panels and wind turbines. Bush is devoting some money to this, there is some investment, but it isn't nearly enough. The green technology sector needs more encouragement."

David was hugely grateful for these insights, not least because it reminded him that some Americans were trying to do things better. It also reminded him that Americans can be quietly spoken. The two men shook hands, exchanged cards and agreed to keep in touch.

23

The express bus for Lusaka was due to leave at 9.00 and David was at the bus station on time, but it was almost 10.00 before the packed vehicle finally left Ndola. The driver seemed determined to make up for lost time. The bus ignored speed restriction signs, screeched round corners with the passengers thrown around, hanging on for dear life, and did the 170 miles to the capital in little over three hours, including stops.

As David hauled his bike from the bus, he decided that he would stay at the Moses Hayward Development Agency if they had a spare bed. He bought a map, but finding the place was not easy. It lay at the foot of a valley, on the banks of a stream, and a little further from the city centre than Grace had suggested. He walked down the steep hill that led to it, rang a door bell and waited, cycle bag in hand. The door was opened by a youngish man whose first words were: "You must be David, we're expecting you. Grace told us you would probably be coming, although we did not expect you for some days yet -- you have done well!"

And David explained that he had not cycled the whole way, by any means, in fact only about 20 miles of it. But there was a bed, he was told, and was made welcome.

"Where's the best bike shop?" he soon asked, "I need a new wheel."

He was accompanied to the shop and explained what he wanted, but the assistant shook his head.

"We will have to get one of those from Jo'berg. Take a week."

A week! It was already late May and David had to be back in London by the end of June. If he was to complete the ride to Cape Town, there would have to be some lifts and trains along the way. But he nodded, there was no option.

He wandered around the city but soon felt tired and went back to his home for the night -- and asked if he could stay for a week. Later that evening he went out for a meal with the head of the Moses Hayward Development Agency, Vincent, a man of about the same age as David. Vincent told him that environmental factors threatened to erode major gains that Southern Africa had made in the past two decades unless urgent steps were taken.

Climate change, the rapid loss of the forests and other natural resources, the damage caused by tourism, all are taking their toll, he said. "The environment is the base for development. Ruin it and development is ruined. It all starts and ends with the environment, with our natural resources. They are the pillar."

Vincent spoke of the difficulties facing environmental organisations in the country and in Southern Africa in general. The region does not have an established climate change movement like India, he said. Foreign corporations are buying up land in the region to grow biofuels, and often causing huge damage. But there are no penalties or fines for the environmental damage they cause.

And NGOs in Zambia are few in number, Vincent went on, while the environmental challenges are huge. Civil society does not yet have the power to significantly influence Zambia's environmental policy. Foreign aid could usefully help the country's NGOs build their capacities at local level -- Western-country NGOs have a wealth of international experience, he pointed out, that local NGOs could learn from.

David was grateful for these insights and also grateful for the use of the agency's computer to check his now numerous e-mails. There was one from Grace, enquiring about his journey. He replied to tell her about his near-death experience.

A week stranded in Lusaka did not appeal very much. But the following morning over breakfast, Vincent handed him an unexpected invite.

"The British High Commissioner has somehow got to know that a British journalist is in town. News travels fast round here. He's holding an early evening garden party at the High Commission today and would like us to go."

David's heart sank. After his encounter with British officialdom in Côte d'Ivoire, he didn't fancy another one. Vincent seemed to pick up his thoughts.

"He's ok, your man here. And it's just a party," laughed Vincent. "And the wine will be good."

The High Commissioner lived in an imposing house, with spacious lawns and high fences, the lawns already full of well-dressed people when the not-so-well-dressed David nervously arrived. White-coated waiters were quietly milling around with trays of drinks.

"Ah, Mr Fulshaw I presume," said the High Commissioner heartily, "I heard about what happened to you and your bicycle. So sorry to hear that. Anyway, you must tell me all about it. Do grab a drink and we'll talk later." David nodded, took a glass of chilled white wine, and was impressed at how good it was.

"Only the best for the Brits," said Vincent quietly, "even though the wine is French." David took another glass, and on a lovely evening in the perfectly-manicured garden, he began to enjoy the occasion. He helped himself to another glass, and also to some tasty nibbles on sticks. And then to another glass. Because he was a new face, and as most people there seemed to know each other well, David began to attract some attention. A small group gathered around him and a man with a ruddy complexion asked him about what he was doing in Africa.

The group listened in stunned silence to David's brief and necessarily sanitised account of cycling on the continent. Everyone looked at him as though he was mad.

"I say," said a lady with a plum in her mouth, "that's amazing, but have you ever fallen orrff?"

David replied that he had never fallen orrff, but that he had been knocked orrff by a lorry which had ruined his front wheel, nearly killed him in the bargain and had not stopped either. More silence followed.

"That lorry driver was a cad, sir, an absolute cad," said the man with a ruddy complexion. David walked around to exchange pleasantries with other guests, including the High Commissioner's wife who seemed positively charming.

"Isn't the High Commissioner a dear," a lady in a long flowing robe, and with the standard issue plum in her mouth, said to David; "he's such a good diplomat. You know what a good diplomat is, don't you? He's someone who can tell you to go to hell in a way that convinces you that you will enjoy the journey!"

As the lady with the robe and the plum laughed uncontrollably at her own joke, David noticed that the High Commissioner was moving in on him. When only a few yards away, however, a white-gloved butler approached the Commissioner, holding out a small silver tray carrying a piece of paper.

"A dispatch from Her Majesty, sir," said the butler in a solemn voice. "I thought that you would want to see it immediately." The High Commissioner read the message, looked up somberly and said: "Oh dear, this is bad news, I will come in straight away."

"Whatever's happened?" David asked Vincent. "Has World War Three broken out?"

"No, the butler does that to impress the guests. It wouldn't be from Her Majesty at all. Probably just from a crony or someone."

A few minutes later, an ashen-faced Commissioner returned. "Really bad news," David heard him say, "we've lost the Test. Routed in the last hour of play. And it was a match we were all set to win. Dreadful outcome."

David helped himself to another glass of wine, and then another. It was the best wine he had downed for months, for years, he mused. I can't afford to buy wine this good, he thought. Then he realised that his taxes were paying for it. When the waiter came over again, David caught sight of the label. It was from Meursault in Burgundy, one of France's most classic white wine villages. It was wine that could cost £20 a bottle in a shop.

The thought that he was helping to pay for it was enough to encourage David to thoroughly misbehave, to take two more glasses of the vintage, and to stagger round the garden with a glass in both hands. But after teetering on the edge of a flower bed, and then falling ignominiously into it, spilling the contents of one glass of the lovely Meursault onto unappreciative flowers, while holding the other triumphantly in the air, a lady perhaps ten years older than David, and wearing a short, slinky dress, lent a hand to pull him out.

"I say, we have maybe had a weeny drop too much of the vino, have we?," said the lady in the short slinky dress.

"Well, me too," said the short slinky dress, "terrible thing alcohol, isn't it? Why, if it wasn't for alcohol, I reckon I'd still be a virgin." At which, two squiffy people were to be seen roaring their drunken heads off at the side of the flower bed.

"I'm not sure I quite believe that," said David eventually.

"No, I don't believe it either, but there is a element of truth in it nonetheless. I'm Fanchon by the way. It's a French name. Friends call me Fanny. David, is it? Yes, I heard about you. David, it is so nice to see a new face at these things. There's a regular circuit here you know. The Brits have a party one week, the French the next, the Chinese the next and so on, even more frequently at times, and there's a weeny bit of competition between them. The Brits try to outdo the French, but they do it by serving -- French wine!"

"But apart from the wine, these parties are so boring, mostly the same old faces. So I only come for the wine," said Fanny, before adding in a slower and more sultry voice, "and for anything else I just might happen to find." Moving closer to David, she purred: "David, you need to recover from your fall. I live close by. Why don't you come back to my place for -- coffee?"

"Thanks, but I don't drink coffee," lied David.

"Good." The short slinky dress moved even closer to David. "I haven't got any coffee! What I do have is a nice empty house. My husband is away on business. You and I could listen to music, and maybe make a little music of our own," said Fanny, moving her hand gently up David's arm.

"I'm sorry but I'm staying with friends, I really have to decline, but thank you for pulling me out of the flower bed," said David as coherently as he could.

"I've obviously failed to pull you into another one. Silly boy." As the disappointed slinky dress moved away, the wine waiters also seemed to have moved away, and people were starting to leave. David too decided that it was time to pull stumps. He stumbled unsteadily out of the garden, managed to avoid the High Commissioner, who was thankfully then busy with another guest, said profound if gabbled thanks to the High Commissioner's wife, and, on the arm of the more sober Vincent, was helped to find his way along the road.

While next morning may have been the morning after the night before, David felt surprisingly good. Must have been because the wine was so good that it didn't give you a hangover, he reasoned. What a sensitive man the High Commissioner was, he decided, as he reflected on the party. "An island of affluence in a sea of poverty," just about summed it up, he thought, and he, David Fulshaw, was part of the island, but how long could the island survive?

"I thought I'd lost you last night," said Vincent over breakfast, "first to the wine, then to the woman. Only the song was missing."

"Sorry I behaved so badly. I enjoyed it in a way. No excuse, but I haven't been to a social occasion like that for almost six months. At first it was like a breath of fresh air compared with some of the things that have happened to me. I guess I took too big a gulp of the air."

Vincent told that him that he could, if he wished, accompany a member of the Moses Hayward Development Agency who was leaving that afternoon to visit a project and would be away for a few days. David leapt at the chance.

"Why don't you stroll round the city this morning, take in the Cathedral perhaps," suggested Vincent, "it's not too far, and well worth a visit. Take my bike. You will maybe have to push it up the hill but then it's flat." David accepted the offer, wheeled out the bike, did his customary check of seeing that the wheels were running free and the brakes worked, and set off.

Lusaka's Anglican Cathedral of the Holy Cross was built in 1957 in the style of Coventry's new Cathedral, David discovered. Its foundation stone was laid by the Queen Mother. The Cathedral opened in 1962, the same year as Coventry.

He locked up the bike and walked inside. The Cathedral was modern, impressive, there were few people around, and David walked into one of the chapels and sat there in silence. He remembered the silence he had experienced with Grace just evenings before, and again he felt moved. He recalled the Greek proverb about no wisdom without silence. He decided that times of silence would in future be part of his life.

Walking by a side door, he heard voices. Going through the door to take a look, he found the voices were coming from a hall. He went in. Some 70 or 80 people were sitting inside and a priest was srolling up and down, talking. A woman at the door smiled, said welcome, and handed David a leaflet. "Questions and Answers Session," it read. He sat down in a side spot and listened to the priest answering a question. As David did not know what the question was, he did not have much idea what the priest was talking about.

When the priest had finished, there was silence for a moment, before a hand went up and a young woman asked the question -- "Why does God allow suffering? As we believe in a loving God, why doesn't God intervene to stop suffering, like

213

stopping the poor dying in pain of disease?" Moments of silence followed the question.

"In this world, we will never have a complete answer to your question," the priest replied, "what we can do is to reflect on the nature of God. To look at what God is like helps us to look at where God is in suffering. And the only accurate picture of God the world has seen is Jesus, God the Son. 'He who has seen me, has seen the Father', said Jesus.

"Jesus suffered on the cross. He went to the cross voluntarily. He suffered and he identifies with the suffering. The cross tells us that God is love, suffering love.

"The cross shows us that God is vulnerable. Jesus, God the son, died on the cross 2000 years ago because people decided that he should die. They exercised their free will. God did not stop them. Why? Because God gives us all a free will. If we choose to exercise that will in a way that is damaging for others, and for ourselves, God does not stop us. He gives us freedom, to choose the right or the wrong path. If we choose the wrong path, it will grieve God's heart, but he does not stop us.

"God does not act like some giant policeman in the sky, stopping us going down a particular road. If we recklessly damage our health, God does not stop us. God guides us to use the free will he gives us in accordance with his will for us. But if we ignore it, if we turn away from God, then we cannot blame God for what happens. The world is not God's puppet theatre. God is vulnerable to our choices, his nature is to be power-less.

"OK, but what about the suffering caused by earthquakes, tsunamis, typhoons, devastating flooding, severe droughts and so on, all of which are happening more and more these days. Where is God in all these disasters? Why doesn't God intervene to stop them?

"For a start, we should stop calling disasters 'natural disasters'. Severe floods and droughts, hurricanes, typhoons and cyclones are occurring at twice the rate of 40 years ago. They are not as natural as they seem, they are more related to the way that people live than they appear. Disasters are increasingly related to changes in weather patterns, to emissions of carbon, to the world's heavy use of energy. And the chief culprits are industrialised countries."

If David had been dozing a little in the warm room, he was suddenly wide awake.

"Climate-related disasters, which kill thousands of people and cost millions in terms of providing aid to stricken populations, are man-made and should no longer be termed natural disasters," said the priest. "What about earthquakes? Well, the damage is not so natural -- 98 per cent of people who die in earthquakes do not die because of the earthquake itself, but because buildings collapse on them. Flimsy buildings are related to poverty. On tsunamis, we know from the tsunami in Asia in December 2004 that where nature's barriers were intact -- mangrove forests along coastlines, for example -- there was far less damage. New tourist hotels, shrimp farms etc had caused many natural barriers to be removed."

"This country is not a major culprit in terms of emissions, but we can nonetheless do what we can to cut our emissions of

215

carbon, our use of electricity, gas and oil. It will help to give our children, our grandchildren a future. And we could maybe persuade any friends and contacts you have in North America and Europe to cut their emissions.

"Where is God in the suffering caused by disasters? God is lamenting the causes of suffering and God is with those who suffer. And God is with us, calling us to be responsible stewards of the beautiful world he created. Next question, please."

David sat there transfixed. Here was a priest persuading Zambian people to cut their carbon emissions even though they were small, tiny, by comparison with the West's, and courteously and correctly pointing to the much larger emissions of industrialised countries. The next question was then put: "Could you explain the precise meaning of a parable?"

"A parable is a story designed to illustrate a truth," the priest replied. He then illustrated his reply with the parable of the Good Samaritan. Another question followed, the meeting ended and David left, feeling humbled by the priest's reply to the question on suffering.

Out of the hall, he unlocked the bike and for some reason, Lydia Green came to his mind. Why, he wondered? Lydia was the last person he wanted to think about. But in a strange way, he sensed an odour, Lydia's odour. He dismissed the thought and cycled past a bustling market to his home for the week.

He reached the top of the hill that led down to the Moses Hayward Development Agency. The hill was steep, the gradient at least per cent. David enjoyed going fast downhill, it was one of the joys of cycling, but he soon needed to apply his brakes. He pressed the brake levers on the handlebars. The brakes not did not respond. To his utter horror, he realised that the brakes had failed, that he had no means of stopping and was now flying down the hill at almost 30 miles an hour.

There were no side roads or turnings that could serve as a escape route. His terrifying options were to put a foot in the front wheel and risk losing this toes, jump off and hope for the best, or go to the foot of the hill and plunge into the stream. In desperation and with some difficulty he jumped off, but it did not go according to plan. He swerved, fell off sideways and banged his head hard against a parked car. The world went blank. He was unconscious.

* * *

For the second time on his African journey, David Fulshaw woke up in a hospital ward.

"Where am I?" he groaned to no one in particular. "Where am I?" He was heard by a nurse not far away.

"You are here, sir, in a hospital in Lusaka. You were brought here earlier by ambulance workers, after you fell off your bike and banged your head very heavily. Your face is a mess, you have a cracked rib, but you're lucky to be alive. Don't try to move, lie still. What's your name, your address? Let's get down some particulars. And who is going to look after you?"

It was a question that was becoming all too familiar, but this time David did have a local contact. He asked the nurse if she would ring Vincent at the Moses Hayward Development

Agency. Maybe someone at the agency would be good enough to look after him. Vincent came into the ward soon afterwards, looking alarmed.

"The bike! The brake cables were cut. Why would anyone want to do that?" said Vincent.

"You are not to get him excited," said the nurse. "He has to rest. Will you look after him?"

"Yes, we will look after him," said Vincent, "what does he need -- food, fresh clothes, medicine?"

"And he has to lie here for at least two days," said the nurse. For two days, Vincent and others from Moses Hayward Development Agency brought him food and spent time with him. The bruised cyclist was then taken back to the agency to recuperate. But not until the nurse warned him that he would unwise to cycle for a month.

This was not advice that David either wanted to hear or intended to take seriously. He e-mailed Peter in Nairobi about the brake cables being cut, and Peter had e-mailed back to say that he was coming from Nairobi with a return ticket for himself and a single Lusaka-Nairobi ticket for David. Grace had also e-mailed him and David had replied to tell her of the CIA plots. Grace urged him to take the medical advice, and added that she was coming to Lusaka to see him. Vincent also warned David that the High Commissioner was likely to call.

As, indeed, he did. "Mr Fulshaw, how good to see you again. I am so sorry to hear what happened to you. Who would want to disable your bike brakes? Someone with a grudge perhaps? Someone you have upset in your newspaper?"

David shook his head and decided not to go into details. He felt he owed the High Commissioner an apology.

"High Commissioner, thank you for coming to see me, it gives me a chance to apologise for my behaviour at your garden party. No excuses, but the wine you served was magnificent. I guess I enjoyed a drop too much."

"Well, thank you for your kind comments about the wine," said the High Commissioner, diplomatically saying nothing about David's behaviour; "It was a Meursault from the village of that name in eastern France. My family has had a modest chateau in the village for some generations. Vines grow on our land and we sell some of the grapes to a local winemaker. In return, we get a good deal on the wine. And by the way, your bike crash was seen by a policeman and I expect the police will be coming to see you."

The High Commissioner had barely left when two policemen arrived. Hands were shaken and the more senior policeman expressed regret for what had happened, but wanted to know about who would have a motive for disabling his brakes.

David did not want to go into the story. His sense of Lydia's odour outside the Cathedral was best kept to himself, he decided. He answered that journalists do write things that some people dislike, but that it was unusual for anyone to go as far as cutting brake cables. The policemen left, David wondering if they realised that they were not getting the whole of it.

24

The laid-off cyclist had no option but to spend several days lying around the Moses Hayward Development Agency to recover. He was soon bored; doing nothing just did not suit him. But at least there was a good library. He picked up a recent addition entitled 'Desmond Tutu: Rabble-Rouser for Peace,' a biography by John Allen. With 496 pages, this should keep me happy for a while, he thought.

The book he found fascinating. In South Africa in the 1980s, Archbishop Desmond Tutu had made a more powerful contribution to the campaign to end apartheid and to free Nelson Mandela than David had realised. And he did it by speaking his mind, boldly. But it was something about half-way through his book that brought David up with a jolt.

Apartheid was as evil and unchristian as nazism, said Tutu. He compared South Africa as it was then to Nazi Germany. He referred to the mass removals of African people, saying: "The gas chambers were probably more efficient and more clean... (but) if you put children in places where you know that they will starve, you are as guilty as those who stoke up the gas chambers."

And that made David think, think a lot. If Western governments pursue policies that cause people in poorer countries to die, if they will not take reductions in carbon emissions seriously, if their policies cause climate change that kills others, then surely those policies can be compared to nazism. For what difference did it make if you starve people by putting them in gas chambers, or starve them by making their climate so inhospitable that they cannot survive? It was a stark thought, but it was surely right, he reasoned. Later that day, he spoke with Vincent about it.

"Well, maybe you are on to something," said Vincent; "there's a verse in the Bible: 'The bread of the needy is the life of the poor; whoever deprives them of it is a murderer. To take away a neighbour's life is to commit murder'. If climate change is denying people the bread they need, if it is stealing people's livelihoods, then yes, the comparison you are making is fair." Which encouraged David to think more about it, and include the comparison in his planned wind-up article from Africa.

Still looking for reading matter, a leaflet on a library shelf caught David's eye. It was headed "JUSTICE IN THE BIBLE." He read through it, pausing to smile at the first paragraph as it was the verse that Grace had mentioned over breakfast. The leaflet read:

How is a just man supposed to act? If you pursue justice, you will attain it and wear it as a glorious robe *(Sirach 27:8).* Blessed are they who observe justice, who do righteousness at all times! *(Psalm 106:3).* Execute justice in the morning, and deliver from the hand of the oppressor him who has been robbed *(Jeremiah 21:11-12).*

221

You shall not pervert justice; you shall not take a bribe, for a bribe blinds the eyes of the wise and subverts the cause of the righteous. Justice, and only justice, you shall follow *(Deuteronomy 16:19-20)*. Give justice to the weak. Rescue the weak and the needy; deliver them from the hand of the wicked *(Psalm 82:3-4)*. Hate evil, and love good, and establish justice in the gate *(Amos 5:14-15)*. Wash yourselves; make yourselves clean; remove the evil of your doings from before my eyes; cease to do evil, learn to do good; seek justice *(Isaiah 1:16-17)*. When justice is done, it is a joy to the righteous, but dismay to evildoers *(Proverbs 21:15)*.

While David found the verses uplifting, again it raised questions. He thought back to that meeting in the Cathedral. As God gives people a free will, and does not stop people doing evil, what is to stop the evil winning over the good, he wondered? How can God bring forth justice to the nations, when powerful interests were bent on injustice? He remembered his conversation over breakfast with Grace. What Grace had said was convincing, but did the powers of injustice have the upper hand, he wondered?

He was not sure whether politicians and the giant corporations who ran the show could share one common, selfless and unconditional love for humanity, that they would want to do justice to the poor and hungry. Such a utopian scenario might be attainable one day, but hardly soon, he thought.

A Bible lay on a table. David opened it at random, at Psalm 119. These words caught his eye: "Do not let the godless oppress me." That's a plea, he thought, that recognises that the godless can oppress people. For godless, read the corporations, he wondered?

222

Peter arrived, looking worried and shaking his head. "It's not just that you're in no fit state to continue your ride. It's that the CIA will not stop until they get you. They will be furious that you have escaped them so far. But you're in danger. After three close shaves, you would be mad to go on. Quit the bike ride while you're still in one piece, David. Come back with me and continue your research in Nairobi." David decided that maybe it was better to stay alive. But when the bike shop rang to say that his new wheel was there, he almost had second thoughts....

In the meantime Grace had arrived. "I've read some of your stories," she told David; "They are a shade vitriolic, you know, but I can sense your anger and yes, you are right to be angry. But don't you think you would make more of an impact with a rather softer approach?"

"The problem with a soft approach on this issue is that no one would take much notice. It's only by being hard-hitting that people sit up and react. While I've been here I've read a biography of Desmond Tutu. He didn't make the impact he did by pussy-footing around. He called evil an evil. I am no Desmond Tutu, but it seems to me that the same principle applies with climate change. I'd love to talk more about it with you. I hope to come back to Zambia soon."

As he prepared to leave Lusaka, David was given another slant on his work by Vincent. "Having read all your articles over the last six months, I think, David, that you are playing the role of an Old Testament prophet. Those prophets were people who cried out against injustice and evil, warning about what would happen if people did not change their ways. That's exactly what you are doing."

"Me, a prophet!" David responded. "You must be joking. I wouldn't imagine that a prophet would disgrace himself at a posh party like I did!"

"Well, the prophets were not perfect people," said Vincent, "and neither were they liked much. Their message was uncomfortable and what they said could apply today. One of them, Isaiah, really laid it on the line. He told people: 'The earth lies polluted under its inhabitants; they have transgressed the laws, violated the statutes, broken the everlasting covenant. The inhabitants of the earth are scorched. The city of chaos is broken down, every house is shut up....all joy has reached its eventide; the gladness of the earth is banished'. "

"Isaiah and other prophets told people they had to change if they wanted to survive, just as you are doing now. People in those days didn't want to know. And I fear, David, that this may happen with your message. People will not want to know. And when they find out that people like you were right all along, that your warnings were spot-on, it may be too late. That's a bleak scenario but I think you should be ready for it."

"Were any of the prophets heard?" David wanted to know.

"While many of the prophets had a difficult time being heard, they could not be ignored. Read the book of Jonah -- Jonah got his message across so powerfully that a whole city was persuaded to change its dubious ways. The greatest of the Old Testament prophets was Moses and he certainly had an impact. He led his people out of slavery. Don't despair, David, keep telling the story you have to tell as you see it. Be faithful to your message. Don't expect results, but don't despair either. Changes may come, I hope they come before it's too late."

224

25

"How did they know where I was all the time?" was the question that David kept on asking when he was back at Peter's flat in Nairobi.

"The CIA has very sophisticated personal monitoring devices," said Peter, "far more sophisticated than most people realise. I've been talking to some personal surveillance experts since you were last here, and from what they have told me, I would not be surprised if the CIA has planted a small device in your stuff."

David's mind went back to the American he had met in the bar at Dodoma. The man had boasted about his personal GPS. Maybe there were such things, he thought. But in his bag, he would have seen it. Where could it be that he wouldn't see it, he wondered.

His radio! The radio was opened up and there, to David's astonishment, was a tiny box that had nothing to do with sound waves.

"That's it!" said Peter, "that is your own personal GPS, planted there by a CIA agent one evening probably, when you were out, tripping the light fantastic, and which tells those guys in Washington D.C. just exactly where you are at all times. This explains how that woman Lydia knew your whereabouts. You didn't know it, but she would have followed you in a car to that hotel where you nearly met your end, checked in a few minutes after you, and bribed the receptionist to let her not sign the guest register."

The two men took a sharp knife and prized the box off the side of the radio.

"Want to keep it as a souvenir?" asked Peter.

"Keep it!" replied David with more than a touch of indignation, "I'm going to take a bloody hammer to it. That thing has nearly cost me my life, three times over!" The device was duly hammered, a device tiny in size, but with great potential to track. Great was its fall into tiny pieces.

As David thought about his wind-up story on the visit, Peter told him: "You should take a look at this. It's an e-mail from a colleague in Uganda. He says that Uganda is sitting on what is potentially the largest onshore oil reserves in sub-Saharan Africa. But once again the story of oil in Africa looks set to be a story of environmental degradation. He says that flares look set to be lit along the shores of the country's Lake Albert, and that corporations and the government cannot be trusted to protect the Ugandan people from the negative impacts of oil extraction. And there's a complete absence of penalties for environmental damage caused by the companies, he claims.

"You might also like to look at the link between climate change and conflict," Peter went on. "Countries where climate change is hitting hard are likely to be countries where there is conflict. Scarce resources have become scarcer and there are fewer to go round. Conflicts over water are common. It's happening in parts of Bangladesh, in Darfur, the Middle East, and the conflicts are likely to increase in number. While climate change alone may not cause conflict, it can accelerate instability or conflict, placing a burden on civilian institutions and militaries around the world."

David took all this on board but wasn't sure he could take on much more. There were so many aspects of climate change, so many ways it was affecting people's lives, so many ways in which companies with power were abusing power.

It was a few days before the end of June. David needed to be back at the paper on Monday, the 2nd of July. On an impulse he said to Peter: "Look, I have a few days in hand. I'd like to end this journey where I started it, in Senegal. I want to go to Dakar and talk if I can with the woman refugee I met, Farna. I will never forget meeting her, she was the first refugee I met. I would love see her again."

"Well, it will be a long flight, take you all day, and you may need two changes, so I suggest you leave your bike in its bag with me," said Peter. "I'm going to London in August so I will bring it with me then."

Leaving Nairobi at breakfast time the next day, it was just after midnight when David arrived in Dakar. After crashing out for the night in an airport hotel, he set out next morning to find Farna. The trouble was, he had only a vague idea of where he had met her some six months beforehand. He decided to go to the city centre hotel where he had then stayed, and see if he could retrace his steps.

Again, he walked along the beach, past the fishing boats, before turning inland to walk through Dakar's narrow streets, along the path he thought he had taken. It led nowhere but to a rubbish dump. He went back, almost to the beach before taking a track with a shop on the corner that he thought he recognised. Again he was wrong. A few warehouses and nothing else lay at the end.

He then remembered that he had walked quite a long way that January day. He sat down with a map and tried to figure it out. At last it came to him, and after a lengthy walk, he found himself in the shanty area where he had met Farna and the children. But where could he find her, he wondered, among the ramshackle huts, tents and other canvas. The tents, the small shacks of wood, tin and other materials all looked so much the same.

As children tugged his sleeves, and a few elderly people held out their hands, David realised that he had no idea where Farna lived. He would have to ask, something he was reluctant to do. Eventually it became inevitable. It also seemed pointless, no one had any idea. But after numerous shaken heads, at last he got a nod, and a woman pointed him up a narrow lane, to "near the top, on the left."

Now he did recognise the lane, and before reaching the tent, was greeted by one of Farna's children. She took David's hand and led him to where her mother was washing clothes at the front of their makeshift home.

A relieved David held out this hand with a -- "I don't suppose you remember me?"

"Yes, of course I remember you. You came earlier this year. You are welcome," said Farna.

Anxious not to pry too much into Farna's life, David began by speaking about his journey, about the people like Farna that he had met, who could no longer make a living in their homes, who had been forced out by matters beyond their control. As David spoke, so neighbours came out of their huts and tents to listen. A small crowd had gathered before Farna began to speak.

"Well, in the six months since you came, life for us has not got any better. My husband finds whatever he work he can, but that is not very often, and we survive on a day-to-day basis, often not knowing where our next meal is coming from, sometimes going the whole day without food, but at least we have survived. Not everyone who came here from our village and from villages near us has survived."

"That's right," chipped in a man standing by Farna, "In the last six months, several people have committed suicide and over a dozen families have died together in poverty. Voluntary agencies give us some help, without them we would be in an even bigger mess, but what we really want is to go back home. But that's not possible, new people are arriving from the villages almost every day and telling us their stories. Here, we have no electricity, no clean water, no drainage system. We have to walk half a mile for water and even then it may not be safe to drink. Our children have very little education because we cannot afford school fees. Employment is limited because the jobs are taken by people who live in the city, as they are better educated. We also face the dangers of fires, as our huts are so close together, and also from disease which spreads very quickly here."

Silence hung in the air. David felt that words from him would be useless at a time like this. He was so moved he was barely able to speak. It was Farna who broke the silence.

"Every day I think about my home, my village, and I can't stop the tears coming to my eyes," she said quietly. David tried but failed to stop tears coming to his eyes.

Back at the hotel, he sat by the window in his room and looked out over the hotel garden to reflect on the whole journey. Six months, six months he had been lucky to survive, six months that had humbled him, six months when victims of climate change had told him what life was like for them, six months that had deepened his understanding of the issues. And yet six months in the life of Planet Earth in the early 21st century when the climate had almost certainly changed, and not for the better.

He reflected on how the events of the last six months, including the attempts to nobble him, had a number of parallels with what was happening in the wider world. He thought back to the Question and Answer session in the Cathedral in Lusaka, and to the question about parables. Was his journey a parable, he reflected? Had it taken on a meaning that he had not envisaged? Did his experiences illustrate a wider truth?

He had cycled through African, a one-man island of affluence on two wheels, riding through a sea of poverty. He had been able to buy the food and accommodation he needed, he could afford to take the train when it suited him, to pay a bribe for his freedom, to invest mony in a refugee to say thanks for the return of his bike.

He thought back to the parable of the Good Samaritan. In that story, a man had been robbed and left half-dead at the side of the road. Two people, good people, had passed by on the other side. David had seen for himself how many people in Africa were being robbed of their land and livelihoods by climate change. Many had been left half-dead. And worse. But affluent people on other shores were passing by, they just did not want to know. They did not want to change the way they live, were not interested in reducing their emissions of carbon. But like the Samaritan, some did care.

A woman had tried to poison him, but who was poisoning the world, he asked himself? All of us, especially us in the West. People had tried to kidnap him, but who was kidnapping the world? Again, all of us. The brakes on his bike had been tampered with. But who was tampering with Planet Earth? He came up with the same answer.

He went back to the afternoon when he was lost in a forest. Lost. The world was lost, would it ever find its way? And David's mind turned to that evening in the High Commissioner's garden when he had disgraced himself. He had teetered on the edge and then fallen into a flower bed. Was the world also disgracing itself, was it teetering on the edge, he wondered, was it staggering around in a drunken state, unable to think coherently about how to get out of the mess that climate change was causing?

"If it wasn't for alcohol, I'd still be a virgin," a slinky lady had said to him. If it wasn't for the way we live, the earth might be a virgin. That evening was a luxury, a luxury enjoyed by rich people behind high fences. The poor were on the other side. But how long would the fences survive, he wondered.

The slinky lady. That sultry voice. Temptation lay all around, thought David, not least the temptation to get on with our own lives and not to be bothered with all this climate change business if we could possibly avoid it.

The High Commissioner with the family chateau in another country. The good deal he was getting that enabled him to serve the best wine. But don't people in the West effectively own lands in poorer countries that give them a good deal, he reasoned, to enable them to live well, don't we all get a good deal? Corporations use their land to grow fruit and vegetables for us, use their labour to make cheap clothes for us, and we invade the sovereignty of poor countries through the way we live. Colonialism, thought David, lives on, but was now repackaged and hidden to make it palatable, something we can live with.

And the cricket! So important, the cricket. But in the game of life, who wins, who loses, depends on where you were born. Who has the chance to eat enough food, to go to school, to have health-care, it's a lottery. And if people who have material wealth are not doing anything to correct that, well, somehow, it just isn't cricket.

He moved away from the window and decided that he had to write his final story while still in Africa.

Let Live

from David Fulshaw, Dakar, West Africa

I have spent the last six months cycling in Africa. Alright for some, you may think, but I can tell you that it was no joyride at times. Don't get me wrong, there were parts of it that I enjoyed enormously. I have met some lovely, generous people along the way, and cycled through some beautiful areas.

But there were other parts of the ride that were rather less happy. Three attempts to nobble me, festering in a police cell on a trumped-up drugs charge, an attempt to steal my bike, a lorry that nearly killed me -- these were among the less happy bits.

I started the journey in Dakar, Senegal and I am ending it here too. My intention back in January was to cycle in Africa to meet people, to go a little deeper, to generally increase my understanding. Well I certainly did all that, but the ride did not work out anything like I could have planned.

Almost from the day I set foot in Senegal, I met people in urban shanty towns who had been forced from their homes, their land, by changes in the climate, by rising temperatures, drought, and extreme weather events. They could no longer make a living in their home villages. The very first displaced person I met was Farna Gomis. And Farna was also the last displaced person that I spoke with, only yesterday. Her family live in a shanty town in Dakar and find it difficult to survive.

In my journey through three countries in West Africa, I met many, many people like Farna. Proud people, hanging on to life for grim death. A grim death is what some of them were facing. Life for Farna has not got any better in the six months since we first met.

In East Africa, many thousands of nomadic people have seen their way of life ruined because of climate change. I have written several articles about them as I have gone along. You will find them on the paper's website.

I have written of the tragedy that is unfolding in parts of Africa, a tragedy of human suffering. What lies behind the suffering? I have to tell you dear reader, that you and I do. It is our heavy use of energy, in our homes, our cars, planes, factories, that is the chief cause of carbon emissions which are casing the climate to change for the worse.

Climate change is an environmental issue, I once thought. No. Rather it is a global justice issue. Rich countries are responsible for almost three quarters of global emissions. But it is poor countries that are bearing the brunt of these emissions. Hundreds of millions face drought, floods, starvation, disease and death.

Here is some of the damage that is happening:
Death: Countless people are already dying each day because of climate change; some figures suggest that it's as high as 160,000 -- a day. They are victims of the West's failure to address climate change in any meaningful way.

Flooding: Vast areas of land will become submerged as sea levels rise with increasing temperatures. Countries such as Bangladesh are already experiencing extreme flooding.

Drought: As temperatures increase so droughts worsen; the food supply of hundreds of millions of people are ar risk.

Disease: With temperatures on the rise, warmer, wetter weather will increase the number of mosquitoes which spread diseases such as malaria. In two of the countries that I rode through -- Kenya and Tanzania -- malaria is already increasing rapidly as a result of the changing climate.

Conflict: A recent report estimates that 46 countries -- home to 2.7 billion people -- will be at high risk of violent conflict due to the combined effects of climate change interacting with others problems. And climate change is turning land into desert and driving people from their homes as I have reported. It is turning proud people into refugees.

The UK Met Office warns that if current trends continue then one-third of the planet will be desert by 2100. Drought is likely to increase globally during the coming century because of predicted changes in rainfall and temperature around the world. At present, according to their calculations, 25 per cent of the Earth's surface is susceptible to moderate drought, rising to 50 per cent by 2100.

The poorest people in the world are the most affected by climate change yet they are the least responsible for it. The rich world is riding on the back of a vast pool of poor people who make only a tiny contribution to carbon emissions. A "Climate Calendar" has been produced by the voluntary organisation, World Development Movement.

The calendar shows by 8th January, just a few days into the new year, the average UK citizen had already emitted as much

CO2 as the average person in one of the 50 least developed countries emits in the whole year. These countries are home to around 750 million people. Eight days, compared with 365 days! For some countries, most importantly the United States, it's worse. In terms of total emissions per year of CO2, for Britain it's 9.62 tonnes per person per year, in the USA it's 20.18 tonnes per person, over twice as much, and the population of the US is five times higher than Britain's.

The US with 5 per cent of the world's population emits 25 per cent of the world's CO2. Almost eight years of George W Bush have given rise to policies which do not accord with the true spirit of those words on the Statue of Liberty, read by countless migrants into the US as they searched for a better life: "Give me your tired, your poor, your huddled masses yearning to breathe free. The wretched refuse of your teeming shore....."

These words are now being shamefully reversed. What is happening today is that masses are huddling into urban slums, innocent victims of climate change. Where is the better life for them? Wretched refugees lie on teeming shores the world over, and the United States has helped to put them there.

Consider the collapse of the Roman Empire. Sixteen hundred years ago Rome was burnt and pillaged by barbarians. It was a profound shock to those who believed that the power of Rome was eternal and God-given. Ring any bells? Powers rise and fall, the US is set for a big fall unless it changes course. Like the Roman Empire it will be unable to defend its interests or cope with its contradictions.

In 2001 the Pentagon admitted that global warming is a destabilising force, that it adds to conflict and puts US troops at risk around the world. It urged that global warming be factored into the country's long term strategic planning. Climate change needs to be factored into all policies that might affect the poor. Insensitive policies and practices should have no place in any country's policies . There's a theory that you can rely on the USA to do the right thing after it has explored all the ways of doing the wrong thing. I hope so. I like American people; I believe they can change, indeed some are already doing so.

It is not only Americans, of course, it is all of us in the Western world. That includes me; I accept that I have contributed to the damage that is being caused. People in the Western world as a whole use cars instead of cycling, walking or using public transport, because they claim that it's more convenient. The fact is that the world is going to hell on this convenience.

When I was recuperating in Zambia from a attempt on my life. I read a biography of Desmond Tutu which made me think. Tutu compared apartheid to nazism, because apartheid was killing people.

But if we do not change the way we live, if Western governments pursue policies that cause people in poorer countries to die, if they will not take reductions in carbon emissions seriously, if their policies cause change that kills, then surely our lifestyles, our government's policies, have the same effect as nazism. For what difference does it make if you starve people by putting them in gas chambers, or starve them by making their climate so inhospitable they cannot survive? It's a stark comparison, and there are differences. As individuals we do not deliberately decide to pursue a lifestyle that makes life harder, even impossible for someone else.

But look at the last 30 or 40 years. As our income in the West has grown so we have bought bigger cars, taken more flights to faraway destinations, used more electrical gadgets etc. But this has all added up to something significant, probably without us realising or recognising it. So it was not a deliberate policy on our part. Nazism and apartheid were of course deliberate policies, but the uncomfortable truth is that the end effect of the way we live today is nonetheless the same as those hideous policies. I believe that we should face up to this.

Climate change is a killer, a weapon of mass destruction, and all of us in the Western world have a hand on the weapon. But as we contributed to the problem so we can do something to solve it. We are all in this together. Farna Gomis's family has been displaced by climate change. When one family is displaced, the entire human race is displaced.

I have been critical of the United States, but I end by quoting an American, Robert F Kennedy: "Each time a person stands up for an ideal, or acts to improve the lot of others, or strikes out against injustice, he sends forth a tiny ripple of hope, and crossing each other from a million different centers of energy and daring, these ripples build a current that can sweep down the mightiest walls of oppression and resistance."

To stop climate change, we must stand up for change. To stop people dying from climate change, we must change the way we live, the way our family lives, and urge our government to change. That way, we will send out ripples of hope that can make a difference. The challenge for all of us in the West is to live in a way that allows others to live. "Let Live" must guide our actions.

Postscript

For his climate change stories from Africa, David Fulshaw was nominated for The Environmental Journalist of the Year Award, 2007. Desspite being the clear favourite, he did not win. His nomination was thought to have been blocked in high places. No. 10 Downing Street was said to be concerned that an award to Fulshaw would send the wrong message to the White House. The special relationship was too important.

In November 2008, Tom Glickmann died of a heart attack, aged 43. It was the day after Barack Obama was elected President. A short time beforehand, Bruce Fieldon was appointed head of a new top-secret intelligence unit in Washington D.C, so top-secret that he never found out what it was doing, or had any idea what he was doing. The unit was disbanded and Fieldon was last heard of in eastern Europe. Heiki Uhempi, alias Lydia Green, is on the run from the police in a number of countries.

David Fulshaw is now based in Zambia as the African environmental correspondent of the London Daily Chronicle. He travels to neighbouring countries by rail, road, and part of the way by bike at times. He is married to Grace of the Moses Hayward Development Agency.

Author's acknowledgements

I would like to thank people I have met in Senegal, Mali, Côte d'Ivoire, Kenya, Tanzania and Zambia whose lives have been affected by climate change, and who shared their stories with me. I am indebted to Panos Institute report "At the Desert's Edge" (a collection of histories of people living in the Sahel) which was helpful for part of Chapter 7. My thanks to Christopher Hall who made helpful comments on an early draft, to Alison Madeley for proof-reading, to Kathy Munns for copy-editing the text, and to Aman Khanna and Carl Rayer.

* * *

If you have enjoyed this book, you can buy a signed copy of John Madeley's novel, Beyond Reach? at a discounted price. Contact john.madeley@gmail.com